When Charles Landon dies the legacy he leaves behind has very different implications for each of his four children. For cynical ZACH LANDON it means a confrontation with EVE PALMER, his father's mistress—and she is quite a surprise!

What *all* Landons find through Landon's Legacy, though, is the key that will finally unlock their hearts....

Dear Reader,

Welcome to the exciting world of the Landons, and to
the legacy that changes the lives of an entire family.

The idea of these books came to me when a friend and
I met for lunch at a restaurant in New York. While we
were waiting to be served, I overheard some women
talking at the next table. They were discussing what
makes a man exciting. "He has to be gorgeous," said
one. "And a rebel," said another. "And not the least
bit interested in being tamed," said a third. The next
thing I knew, Cade, Grant and Zach Landon sprang
to life inside my head. They were certainly handsome,
rebellious and untamable, and when I wonder what
kind of women could possibly put up with them, their
beautiful sister Kyra materialized and said, well,
she'd always loved them, even if they were impossible!

This month I'm delighted to introduce Zach Landon
in *Hollywood Wedding*. Zach thinks he's got no
worlds left to conquer...until *his* world is turned
upside down by the exquisite Eve Palmer, a woman
who's not afraid to tell any man where to get off.

So settle back and enjoy four months of love, laughter
and tears as you discover the full meaning of the
Landon Legacy.

With my very warmest regards,

Sandra Marton

SANDRA MARTON

Hollywood Wedding

Harlequin Books

TORONTO • NEW YORK • LONDON
AMSTERDAM • PARIS • SYDNEY • HAMBURG
STOCKHOLM • ATHENS • TOKYO • MILAN
MADRID • WARSAW • BUDAPEST • AUCKLAND

ISBN 0-373-11819-8

HOLLYWOOD WEDDING

First North American Publication 1996.

PROLOGUE

ZACH hadn't been sure which he wanted most, the woman or the mountain.

The woman had been watching him last night, sitting at a corner table in the inn's lounge and giving him long, slow looks from under her lashes. There'd been no mistaking the message, but after a minute Zach knew it was no contest.

She was beautiful, but the world was full of beautiful women. The mountain was the challenge, all seven thousand, snow-covered feet of it. It would come first.

So he'd smiled back, told the bartender to send her a drink and lifted his glass to her before finishing the last of his brandy. Then he'd strolled toward the door, pausing beside her table.

"Here for the weekend?" he'd asked and when she'd nodded in assent, he'd smiled. "Alone?"

Her tongue had slicked across her lips. "No," she'd murmured, "but that won't stop you, will it?"

Zach had felt his body tighten in anticipation.

"Tomorrow evening," he'd said softly, and then he'd gone to his room, taken a long, cold shower and turned his thoughts to the next day.

Now, as he undid his bindings and stepped out of his skis, he knew he'd made the right choice. His hands were numb with the cold that had managed to seep through his Gore-Tex gloves, his lungs cried out for more oxygen, and every muscle in his body ached.

He felt terrific.

A smile eased across his face, softening the hard, handsome angles and chiseled features.

He could see the copter approaching, skimming up the windswept Himalayan valley like a prehistoric bird, and he pumped a fist high into the air as it began its descent.

The Valley of the Gods had turned out to be perfect, exactly as Elise had promised. Zach grinned, remembering the conversation with his travel agent the week before.

He'd phoned her from the chartered jet, halfway between a dull breakfast meeting at the Boston Club and a duller luncheon appointment at Windows on the World atop the towering World Trade Center in New York.

"I want to get away for a couple of days," he'd said without preamble. His administrative assistant had shoved a stack of papers under his nose. Zach had switched the phone to his other ear while he scrawled his initials on the pages. "Got any suggestions?"

Elise, who'd been dealing with Zach long enough to know exactly what the question meant, had instantly offered several in the British accent she still cultivated after better than forty years in the States.

What did he think of rock climbing in Yosemite? Rafting in Idaho? Sky diving in British Columbia?

"No," Zach had said to each idea, "no, no. I want— I want... Just keep on going," he'd said in exasperation.

Elise had rattled off more proposals while the jet banked over Manhattan's narrow canyons. Zach had listened, frowning as he gazed out the window, picturing himself in an hour's time seated at a table with half a dozen men twenty years his senior who'd pretend they'd really choose grilled tuna and braised radicchio over the rare steaks and butter-dripping baked potatoes their high-priced cardiologists had made them swear off forever, who'd talk stocks and bonds and investments with the appetite and passion most men reserved for women.

Something had knotted in Zach's flat belly.

"Helicopter skiing," he'd said into the phone, cutting short Elise's description of windsurfing in the Caribbean. "Yeah, I know I've done it before, but that was in the Canadian Rockies or maybe it was Alaska. Where? The Himalayas?" For the first time in days, Zach had smiled. "Okay, babe," he'd said, "that sounds good. Let's go for it."

Now here he was, on the far side of the world with a glacier and a mountain all to himself. With half a dozen glaciers and mountains all to himself, and nothing to remind him of the world he'd left behind, the telephones and fax machines and computers, the fat cats and fatter corporations that increasingly demanded his expertise and his time in a game that had grown dull.

Zach puffed out his breath. Here he was, as free as he'd been seven years ago, before he'd let the world suck him in, before he'd traded risk for wealth and freedom for the disaster that had been his marriage, and it felt damned wonderful.

Two hundreds yards away, the copter was settling to the earth in a whirling blizzard of rotor-driven snow. The pilot would probably want to take off right away, considering the lateness of the hour, the bitter cold and the omnipresent danger of avalanche.

Zach knew he'd pushed things to the edge as it was, fast-talking the guy into leaving him on the top of the mountain with nothing but his equipment, an avalanche transceiver, a flask of hot coffee and a couple of thick sandwiches for company.

"I dunno," the pilot had said, scratching his head, "most people go up there with a guide."

But Zach had persisted. The day he couldn't talk his way into or out of a situation hadn't dawned yet. He'd presented his skiing credentials as he would have presented a block of blue-chip stocks for the president of a multibillion-dollar bank and finally the man had shrugged, muttered something about it being Zach's neck, not his, revved the engine, increased the pitch of the blades and left him to the gods and the mountain.

The day had been incredible. And, Zach thought with a start of surprise as he scrambled into the copter, it wasn't over yet.

Someone was waiting for him. It was the woman from last night, dressed in a skintight spandex ski suit that showed off every inch of her lush body.

Zach smiled as he sat down beside her and put his lips to her ear so he could be heard over the noise of the copter.

"What a pleasant surprise."

She smiled back. "I thought it would be."

At least that was what he thought she said. It was impossible to hear, but then, what did a man really need to hear when he was gazing into a pair of thickly fringed amber eyes set above a deliciously turned-up nose and a pouting mouth?

She moved closer, lay a scarlet-tipped hand on his arm and brought her lips to within a breath of his ear.

"I hope you don't mind. I talked your pilot into taking me along while he collected you."

Zach's smile tilted as her thigh settled gently against his.

"Mind? Hell, no. I'm delighted." The helicopter rose into the air and Zach leaned closer. "My name is—"

"You're Zachary Landon. I know." She smiled. "I'm Keri."

Zach drew back so he could look at the soft, smiling mouth that promised paradise, at the high thrust of the breasts that made a man's hands ache to touch them. A surge of desire flooded through him and he pulled the woman into his arms and kissed her.

A man would have to be crazy to turn down a woman like this. She was beautiful and she would sleep with him simply because she enjoyed it. She wasn't like his ex-wife, who used sex for gain. And if she didn't believe in fidelity any more than the former Mrs. Landon had, at least she hadn't taken any vows pretending she did.

Keri's hand began to trace a path up his thigh. Zach caught her fingers in his, and she gave him a slow, dazzling smile before she arched toward him and put her lips to his ear again. Her breath danced along his skin.

"He's gone," she said. "I sent him away."

There was no need to ask who, or what, she was talking about. Zach smiled as he brushed his lips against hers.

"Good," he said, his mouth against the pink shell of her ear, "just so long as you understand that I'll be gone, too, in a week."

Her smile was sexy, her fingers cool as she clasped his face in her hands and drew it close to hers.

"But what a memorable week it's going to be," she said.

Zach kissed her again, more deeply this time, and then he drew her close and gazed out the open door as the helicopter swept across the valley.

Today, he had claimed the mountain. Tonight, he would claim the woman. And if he was lucky, he would not tire of either until it was time to return to the real world. He would go back to Boston, to the house on Beacon Hill and to the brokerage firm that bore his name.

Any man not satisfied with all that was nothing but a fool.

Thirteen hours and another world away, Eve Palmer yawned as she made her way across the dark, silent courtyard of her Los Angeles apartment complex to her front door.

It was two in the morning and she was tired to the bone.

She had risen before six, fought the freeway traffic in her beautiful but ailing sports car and taken the first of a day's worth of meetings at eight. Ten hours later, she'd grabbed a sandwich while she viewed the dailies of Triad's current movie-in-progress, a dog of a film she'd inherited from her predecessor.

At nine o'clock she'd fixed her makeup, slapped a smile on her face and gone to a cocktail party. At eleven, she'd let Dex Burton, Hollywood's newest up-and-coming macho male lead, whisk her off for a late-night supper so they could talk business. At least, that was what Dex had claimed.

Eve made a face as she jabbed her key into the lock of the front door and stepped into her tiny living room. But the only business Dex had wanted to do was in bed.

"You give a little, you get a little, lover," he'd said, flashing her a toothy grin.

It had infuriated her but it hadn't surprised her. She'd learned the lesson early, that men saw nothing wrong in trading power for sex. If it was more obvious in Hollywood than it had been in foster homes back in Minnesota, it was only because Hollywood had more powerful men and beautiful women per square mile than any other place on the planet.

Eve had managed to keep smiling, to pretend she didn't understand Dex's sleazy message. But when his hand had slipped under the table and slid casually up her thigh, her self-control had vanished. She'd told Dex what he could do with his charm and his nonexistent talent, and now here she was, still without a lead for *Hollywood Wedding*, the film that would determine the course of Triad's future, and hers.

The apartment was warm and stuffy. Eve kicked off her shoes and headed straight for the air conditioner, sighing as the first cool blast came sweeping through the vents.

A shower, then bed, she thought as she took off her jacket. It wasn't just the long day that had tired her, it had been standing around at that cocktail party, putting on a bright face to convince the world that rumors of Trident's imminent demise were exaggerated.

At least the other rumors had eased off, the ones that had plagued her after fate had brought Triad into her life.

No. That wasn't quite accurate, Eve thought as she undressed. It wasn't fate that had handed her the top spot at Triad. It was Charles Landon, and that was why the rumors had flown.

Struggling film-production companies were as common as crabgrass, but for a multimillionaire to put a woman at the head of such a company when she had never held that kind of job before—that wasn't common at all.

That Charles had done it on little more than a whim was something the rumormongers couldn't comprehend. In her better moments, Eve had to admit it was hard to blame them. She'd had trouble comprehending it herself, she thought as she pulled the clips from her hair.

Her chin lifted in an unconscious gesture of defiance as a cascade of pale golden curls tumbled down her back.

But her relationship with Charles had been strictly business. She had not wangled responsibility for Triad from an old man in some cheap game played out between satin sheets. She had simply been in the right place at the right time, and Charles had taken it from there.

Sometimes she'd been tempted to stand up in a place like Spago's, bang on a water glass and announce that to the world.

But she never had.

One of life's most painful lessons was that denying a lie sometimes only gave it the aura of truth.

Eve had learned that at seventeen, when her foster father had tried to molest her. After months of complaining, someone had finally believed her. Eve had almost wept with relief, but it had been short-lived. Her foster father had pointed an accusing finger at her and convinced his wife and the social worker that it was Eve who'd come on to him.

No, Eve thought as she switched on the bathroom light, no, there was no point in denying the rumors about

Charles and her. Ignoring them had been the right thing. The whispers had faded, then died—to be replaced by whispers about Triad and speculation about how long the company would take to fail.

But it wasn't going to fail. She wouldn't let it. *Hollywood Wedding* would save Triad, Eve was sure of it. All she needed was the right cast and location....

The breath sighed from her lungs. All, she thought with a little laugh, all.

Eve lifted her head and looked into the bathroom mirror. Her weary smile faded as she met her own cool-eyed gaze. She could do it. She *would* do it. Charles Landon had handed her a once-in-a-lifetime chance, and she wasn't going to let it slip away.

Absolutely nothing, and no one, was going to keep her from succeeding.

Deep in the Himalayas, Zach and Keri entered the inn.

"I'll meet you in the lounge for drinks and dinner after I've showered," he said, with a little smile.

Keri linked her arms around his neck.

"Wouldn't you rather shower in my room?" she whispered. "I'll phone down for champagne, and——"

"Mr. Landon?" Zach turned. The innkeeper stood a few feet away, his expression solemn. "Sir, this just came for you over the wireless."

Zach smiled as he took the message from the man's outstretched hand.

"Don't look so down in the mouth, Patel. Unless it's my office wiring me that the market's crashed..." His voice faded to silence as he scanned the slip of paper again. When he looked up, his smile was gone. "Hell," he said softly.

Keri frowned. "What's the matter?"

Zach ignored her. "I'll need access to your wireless," he said sharply to the innkeeper. "And I'll expect the copter to be ready to leave in five minutes."

"Of course, Mr. Landon. I'm terribly sorry, sir. May I offer my condolences?"

"Zach?" The woman's voice called after him as he hurried up the stairs. "What's happened? Where are you going?"

He paused at the top of the steps and looked down at her, his expression blank. Her name had gone clear out of his head.

"Sorry," he said, "but I'm afraid our plans are off."

A pout spread across her pretty face. "What do you mean, off? You said——"

"I've got to fly back to the States. I just got word that my old man died."

"Oh. Oh, I'm so sorry."

She waited. Zach knew he was supposed to show something, to feel something. But it was too late for that. It was years too late.

All there was time for now was the long journey home.

CHAPTER ONE

SOMEWHERE above the Rocky Mountains, the wild cry of a hawk rose on the early morning air. The sound awakened Zach instantly, just as it always had when he was a boy.

He lay back against the pillows. But he wasn't a boy now, he thought wryly, he was a man, and as free as the hawk. There was no need to dream of the day he, too, could leave behind the Landon mansion and the valley it commanded.

He had done that, thirteen long years ago, and though he had returned from time to time, he had never missed this place.

With a sigh, he shoved aside the blankets, sat up and scrubbed his stubbled face lightly with his hands.

What time was it, anyway? He peered at the clock beside his bed. Six thirty-seven, said the unblinking red digital face. Zach groaned softly and put his head in his hands.

If he was at home in Boston, he'd have already been up half an hour. By now, he'd be shaved, showered and dressed; he'd be on his way downstairs to the sun room, where Howell would greet him with a polite good morning, a pot of freshly ground coffee and copies of the *Boston Globe,* the *New York Times* and the *Wall Street Journal.*

But he wasn't in Boston, Zach thought as he rose to his feet and padded, naked, to the window. He was in

Colorado. And getting up at six o'clock was no pleasure when you hadn't gone to bed until someplace after two the night before.

A grin crept across Zach's face. The evening had been terrific, though. Sitting around, talking and reminiscing with his brothers, was always great.

It never failed to amaze him just how easily he, Cade and Grant fell back into the patterns of their childhood when they got together. Though they were separated by time, by geography and by the demands of their very different professions, all they had to do was meet under the same roof and the years fell away. They were kids again, not just brothers but best buddies, joined by blood, by love—and by their determination to stand up to the common enemy. Their father.

The smile slipped from Zach's face. The enemy was gone now. Charles had been dead almost a week, the funeral was over, and he still didn't feel anything. Hell, you were supposed to feel something when you watched your old man's coffin settling alongside your mother's in the family mausoleum, weren't you, something more than a faint sense of regret?

He shook his head as he ran his hand through his chestnut-colored hair. His brothers had been as stony-faced as he. Kyra had been the only one of the Landon children whose eyes had glittered with tears, but then, his baby sister was as sweet and tenderhearted a soul as had ever lived. That she'd never been one of the old man's victims, Zach thought wryly, proved that there was a merciful God. Charles's tyrannical callousness, his authoritarian coldness, had been reserved for his sons alone.

With a sigh, Zach turned away from the window and headed for the attached bathroom. That was all in the past now, he thought as he stepped into the shower stall, and not just because the old man was gone. Charles had lost power over his sons a long time ago. Cade had escaped at twenty-one, giving up the life the old man had picked out for him for the dream of striking it rich in the oil fields. Grant hadn't lasted that long; he'd made his move at eighteen, going off to the university of his choice instead of his father's and making his way through it and law school on his own.

Zach smiled tightly as he turned his face up to the water. But he'd had less patience than either of his brothers. At seventeen, he'd walked away from this place and...

He laughed. Hell, no. He hadn't walked away, he'd driven—in his father's Porsche. Taking off in the hundred-thousand-dollar car had been his final act of defiance, a kind of in-your-face present from him to Charles as if to prove he was every inch the no-good punk the old man said he was.

Actually, by then, a punk was exactly what he'd become. His grades—except for science, which he loved, and math, which he could do without thinking—were in the toilet. He'd been running with a fast and loose crowd, and it had only been a matter of time before he'd have gotten in trouble with the law.

His smile faded as he stepped out of the shower. Even at seventeen, he'd hated himself for what he was turning into, but he couldn't seem to stop.

Nothing he did was good enough to please his father. His As in math and science didn't make up for the Bs (and occasional Cs) he got in dull subjects like social studies and languages. His position on the football team as a grunting, hurt-in-the-dirt lineman was nothing compared to the flash and dash he'd have had as a running back or a wide receiver. And his friends were the wrong ones, local boys instead of snot-nosed brats from the exclusive school the old man insisted he attend in Denver.

By the time Zach had reached the age of seventeen, it was as if he'd become determined to live down to each of Charles's expectations.

"You'll never amount to anything," Charles had said, for as long as Zach could remember.

Looking back now, Zach had to admit that it might have been true. He never would have amounted to anything, not if he'd stayed in this house.

But the last angry blowup had tipped the scales. It had started over some flippant remark he'd made and quickly escalated to a summary of all Zach's sins. At the end of it, Charles had given him an ultimatum.

"Either you live by my rules or you'll get out," he'd shouted.

Zach hadn't hesitated. Seconds later, he was out the door and in the Porsche, burning rubber as he roared down the driveway and onto the narrow road that led off the estate, driving hell-bent-for-leather into Denver, never stopping until he pulled up at the Army recruitment office.

A smile twisted across his mouth as he recalled the way the scowling recruiting sergeant had looked him up and down, sucked in his cheeks and asked how old he was.

"Eighteen," Zach said, without blinking.

"Eighteen, huh?" The sergeant smiled. "Tell you what, kid. You bring me your birth certificate and we'll talk about enlistment."

The Marine recruiter down the street wasn't as picky, especially because Zach, wiser if still not older, had paused just long enough to get his hands on a doctored driver's license before he put in an appearance.

The Marine had looked at Zach, then at the license.

"You got a birth certificate to back this up, son?" he'd drawled.

"Yes, sir," Zach had answered. It wasn't a lie, not when you considered that his order for the certificate was already in the works.

"And you'll produce it tomorrow?"

"Yes, sir," Zach had said again, his posture erect and his green eyes firmly fixed on the wall just beyond the Marine's head.

The recruiter had shrugged and shoved a stack of papers across his desk.

"Read 'em, sign 'em, and we're in business." As Zach had reached for the papers, the man's callused hand slapped down hard on his wrist. "Just be sure you know what you're doing, son."

Zach had pulled his hand loose and looked up, his eyes suddenly the color of a storm-tossed ocean.

"I'm not anybody's son," he'd said coldly, "and I know exactly what I'm doing."

But, Zach thought now, he hadn't known a damn. He smiled ruefully as he began dressing. Boot camp and Parris Island had seemed a worse hell than the one he'd escaped—except that at the end of it, the Corps had welcomed him to its bosom in a way his father never had.

For the first time in his young life, Zach had found a home.

By the time he left the Marines four years later, he had a sense of discipline, a yearning for success and a twenty-thousand-dollar stake. On two continents and in half a dozen Corps barracks, his take-no-prisoners attitude, coupled with his head for numbers, had turned him into a steady winner at high-stakes poker.

After that, it was easy. The money had seen him through a couple of years of college, where his finance courses had taught him two things.

The first was that he knew more by instinct about stocks and bonds and market shares than his professors.

The second was that playing poker wasn't all that different from playing the markets, it was just that the markets paid off bigger.

At twenty-three, Zach had left school. He'd dabbled in arbitrage for a year, in high-risk corporate takeovers for another. At twenty-five, with a couple of million dollars under his belt, he'd decided to settle down. He'd bought himself a seat on the Exchange.

Now, at thirty, he was head of his own firm, one of the most successful young stockbrokers in America.

And one of the most bored.

Zach frowned and paused with his hand on the hanger that held one of the three almost identical dark blue suits he'd had Howell express here from Boston. It was the truth. He was bored out of his mind. It was terrible to admit, but if there'd been one benefit to this last week, it was that it had, at least, ripped him away from the unvarying routine of his days.

He shook his head. What was the matter with him? He'd come here straight from the Himalayas, where he'd been anything but bored, skiing a mountain that pierced the clouds and making it—well, almost making it—with...with whatever her name had been.

What he needed was to get back to work. He *had* to get back to work. There were fat-cat clients to wine and dine, a dozen dull meetings to chair....

"Hell," he said, under his breath, and he reached quickly past the three suits, hanging shoulder to shoulder like the three Marx Brothers, pulled out the Harris tweed jacket he'd taken with him to the Himalayas and strode from the bedroom.

The house was quiet, just as it had always been. Even when he and Cade and Grant were kids, they'd tried not to make any noise here, automatically saving their rough-and-tumble for the stables or the endless lawns and pastures. There was something about the Landon mansion, Zach thought as he made his way down the wide staircase, that didn't inspire the sound of childish voices lifted in glee.

It didn't inspire the sound of voices at all, he thought, his mouth tightening. The dozens of guests who'd come back here after the funeral had stood around whispering to each other, and there'd been no doubt in Zach's mind that it was the house they were deferring to and not the occasion.

What an incredible circus the funeral had been! Judges, politicos, bankers, CEOs and board presidents from damned near all the Fortune 500 companies in the West had shown up, all of them looking solemn—and all of them trying to figure out which Landon son was the one who was going to take Charles's place.

A smile tugged at Zach's lips as he followed the wonderful aroma of Stella's coffee toward the dining room. What would all those bigwigs say when they learned that they wouldn't have the chance to genuflect to any of the Landons? Yesterday, after the reading of their father's will, the brothers had taken all of two minutes to agree that not a one of them wanted any part of Landon Enterprises.

Zach would check out Landon's corporate worth and put a price on its head. Grant would handle the legal end. Cade would decide which lost and forgotten, poverty-stricken dots on the map were most in need of hospitals and schools, courtesy of the sale.

And that would be the end of it. Charles Landon's gift to his sons would go the way of the dodo bird, a fate it surely deserved. Zach and his brothers would be free; only Kyra would keep any ties to the old man, but that was as it should be.

His face softened as he thought of his sister. She was a sweetheart, the light of all their lives. He could hear her voice now, soft and musical, drifting from the dining room.

"...still can't believe Father left the place to me," she was saying.

Zach smiled as he stepped into the room.

"Why wouldn't he have?" He dropped a kiss on the top of her head and made his way toward the coffee urn. "You adore this place, baby. It would have been wrong if he'd left it to anyone else."

Kyra looked up and smiled. "Well," she said, "don't you look handsome this morning."

Zach smiled back at her, even if it wasn't easy to do. Of all the gloomy rooms in the house, he'd always disliked this one the most. He'd suffered through endless inquisitions and endless criticisms at that big mahogany table.

It suddenly seemed like old timesthe dark furniture, the sideboard overladen with food no one would eat. Lord, he couldn't wait to get out of this place.

He looked at Cade, who was seated at the table with a cup of coffee in his hands.

"Where's Grant?" Zach shot back his cuff and looked at his watch. "I thought he'd be back from that meeting with the old man's administrative assistant by now."

Cade cocked an eyebrow and got to his feet. "And a charming good morning to you, too."

"It's late, in case you hadn't noticed. I've got an eleven o'clock flight to Boston."

"And you're going to make it out of uniform?" Cade shook his head. "I thought all you banker types signed a pledge that said you had to go around in pinstripes."

"I'm not a banker, I'm a stockbroker. And go ahead, pal. Laugh all you want. Just remember that in a couple of days you'll be smiling prettily at an English version of me, trying to convince him to invest in your latest search for maybe-it-exists-and-maybe-it-doesn't oil in— where'd you say you were going this time?"

"The North Sea," Cade said. "And there's no maybe about it, my friend. It's at least as sure a bet as those investments you push."

Zach smiled at the familiar banter.

"Yeah?"

"Yeah. And I suspect that if your fat-cat clients knew I could still beat you arm wrestling without breaking a sweat——"

"Still? What do you mean, still? You never beat me, not once."

"Prove it."

"My pleasure. Just let me take off my jacket and——"

"Dammit, what is this? Are we kids or adults?"

The Landons all swung toward the door. Grant was standing just inside the room, glaring balefully.

"Grant?" Kyra said. "What's wrong?"

Grant tossed a manila folder on the table, strode to the sideboard and poured himself a cup of coffee.

"Nothing's wrong."

A lie if ever I heard one, Zach thought. Grant looked like a man who'd just had the ground cut out from under him.

"Well?" Cade asked. "What did Bayliss want to talk about?"

Grant's lips compressed. "Trouble."

"Trouble?" Zach frowned. "What sort of trouble?"

"This sort," Grant said.

He took the folder from the table, drew two stacks of papers from it and handed one to each of his brothers. Kyra looked at him as if she was waiting for him to hand her something, too. When he didn't, she turned away and walked slowly to the window.

The minutes passed while Zach and Cade leafed through the papers Grant had given them. Finally, Cade looked up.

"What is this crap?"

"Exactly what it seems to be. Father bought an oil company in Dallas——"

"You mean, he bought a disaster." Cade tossed the papers he'd been reading on the table. "And he let it go from bad to worse. Now it's damned near bankrupt."

Zach looked up and frowned. "Oil company? Hell, man, what are you talking about? What I've got here is an acquisitions profile on some two-bit Hollywood production company named Triad. The old man saddled Landon Enterprises with it, and now it's about to sink like a stone."

"You've each got different reports drawn up by Bayliss, but the bottom line's the same. Father bought these companies not long before he took ill, and they seem to have gotten lost in the shuffle."

"Yeah," Zach said, "well, when this Triad outfit goes down for the third time, it's going to take lots of Landon dough with it."

"The same for Gordon Oil," Cade said. "Landon's gonna take a nasty hit when it dies."

Grant's expression grew even more grim. "Terrific," he snarled. "Landon went into the two firms to bail them out. Instead, we seem to have made them worse."

Cade's brows rose. "What do you mean, 'we', big brother?"

"Exactly what I said. As of yesterday, *we* are Landon Enterprises. And we will be, until we find a buyer."

Zach looked at Grant, then at the papers he'd dumped on the table.

"Hell," he muttered, as he gathered them up.

There was no point in arguing with Grant's assessment. He was right, and the three of them knew it. If the Hollywood outfit and that Dallas company went belly up, they'd leave a blotch of red ink on Landon

Enterprises' ledgers big enough to scare off any potential buyer.

Something had to be done, and quickly.

"Okay," Cade said, "tell Bayliss——"

"Bayliss retired, as of this morning." Grant smiled at the looks on his brothers' faces. "He said he was too old to face another Colorado winter. He bought himself a house in the Virgin Islands. He's going to spend the rest of his days on the beach, sipping piña coladas."

Zach cleared his throat. "I'll phone Goodwin, then. Bayliss's second in command. He can——"

"Goodwin's tied up with a dozen other things."

Cade tossed the Gordon Oil report onto the table. "Terrific," he snapped. "What are we supposed to do now?"

"Oh, for heaven's sake!" The men swung around. Kyra was glaring at them as if she couldn't believe what she'd been hearing. "What's the matter with you guys? Are you dumb, or what?" She shook her head. "And don't waste your breath telling me I don't know what I'm talking about. A child could figure this mess out!"

"Kyra," Zach said gently, "baby——"

"You're the financial whiz in this family," Kyra said, stabbing a finger in his direction. "You could fly out to the coast, take a look at Triad's books and decide what can be done to help it."

"Me? Don't be silly. I've got people waiting for me in Boston. I can't just——"

"And you," she said to Cade, "the genius who knows all about oil… Would it be too much to hope that maybe, just maybe, you might be the one to check things out in Dallas?"

"Impossible! I've business in London. I can't——"

"She's right," Grant said. "You two could get a handle on things faster than anybody else."

There was a moment's silence. Cade and Zach looked at each other, and then Zach threw up his arms in defeat.

"Two days," he snapped, "and not a second more."

Cade blew out his breath. "Yeah. Two days, and then... Wait just a minute." He swung toward Grant. "What about you? Don't tell me you're the only one of us who gets to walk away from this mess?"

Color rose in Grant's cheeks. "Not exactly. It seems a friend of Father's named him guardian of his kid a couple of years ago."

Zach and Cade began to smile. "Don't tell me," Cade said.

"Listen, we can change jobs, if you want. The twelve-year-old for the oil company or the Hollywood studio...?"

"No," Zach said quickly, "no, that's okay, pal. I'll deal with Hollywood, Cade'll handle Dallas." His lips twitched. "And I bet you're going to make one hell of a terrific baby-sitter."

Cade tried not to laugh, but a sound burst from his lips. Grant swung toward him.

"This is not funny," he choked.

But it was, and they all knew it. The brothers began to laugh, and then they moved into a tight circle, clapped each other on the back and joined right hands as they had when they were boys.

"To the Deadeye Defenders," they said solemnly. They grinned happily at each other, and then Cade sighed.

"Time to get started."

Zach nodded. "Yeah. I'll see you guys before I leave."

He punched Grant lightly in the shoulder, snapped an imaginary right hook at Cade's chin, blew a kiss to Kyra and made his way to his room to pack.

It was going on ten o'clock. If he was going to make that eleven o'clock flight to Boston...

Actually, it made more sense to fly straight out to California. He was halfway there already; besides, if he went to Boston, he'd only get tied up in a dozen things. And this mess the old man had created had to be dealt with now, not next week or next month.

With a sigh, he sank down on the edge of his bed and scanned the report again. Triad had been privately owned by a man named Tolland. It had never made any real money, although it had at least been able to keep its head above water. About three years ago, its puny profits had finally turned to losses.

Charles had bought the company some months ago. As for who was running it for him... Zach frowned. It was a woman named Eve Palmer, and she had to be doing a piss-poor job because Triad was in its death struggles.

Zach stuffed the report into his suitcase, locked it and reached for the phone. He'd call the office, ask for more detailed info to be delivered by courier to the airport.

While he was at it, he'd make a couple of other calls, including one to Howell telling him to pack something besides those damned dark blue suits and express them to L.A. as soon as he had his hotel arrangements squared away. And his portable computer—he'd need that, too. It was obvious, now that he'd read the report more carefully, that two days on the coast was optimistic.

But five days would surely do it. Triad was dying, and he had dealt with dying companies before, back in the early days when he'd made fast money by moving in and administering the *coup de grace*.

Zach picked up his suitcase, walked briskly to the door and stepped out into the hallway.

By this time next week, Triad Productions would be history.

CHAPTER TWO

IT WAS the kind of day that made people happy they lived in southern California. The sky was blue, the sun was bright, and the temperature hovered in the gentle seventies.

"Fantastic," said the tourists outside Disneyland.

"Terrific," said the roller bladers on Ocean Front Walk.

"Awesome," agreed the surfers at Redondo Beach.

"Rats," muttered Eve Palmer as she sat trapped in bumper-to-bumper traffic. Her car had not moved a mile in the past twenty minutes. The only thing moving was her temper, and it was rising as rapidly as the temperature inside the car.

Whatever had happened to simple things, like windows you rolled up and down at will? Her old Chevy had had them; you could let in air with a crank of the wrist. But this car that Charles had insisted on buying for her did not. Eve had not wanted it. She didn't need a silver car that looked like a Batmobile, she'd told him, but Charles had disagreed.

"The head of Triad must look prosperous," he'd said, as he'd handed her the keys to a vintage Jaguar.

The car had, at first, won her over with its simple but elegant styling. But it was also a money-eating monster, as she'd discovered last week, when the windows, air-conditioning and engine had all begun to malfunction.

A white-coated technician named Hans, looking more like a surgeon than a mechanic, had poked and prodded at its innards. Finally, in hushed tones, he'd pronounced the patient ill but repairable—to the tune of three thousand dollars and three weeks in the shop.

Fortunately for Eve, he'd misinterpreted her sudden pallor.

"If doing without your automobile will be a hardship, Miss Palmer, we can provide you with a temporary replacement."

Eve had opened her mouth, ready to tell him that the hardship would be coming up with three thousand bucks in this lifetime, but then she'd remembered the second thing that Charles had taught her.

"Never let 'em see you sweat," he'd said.

So she'd smiled, shoved her oversize sunglasses off the bridge of her small, straight nose and up into her blond hair and said that it just wouldn't do, not when she was about to begin filming *Hollywood Wedding*.

"With Dex Burton," she'd added, because that was an axiom she'd figured out herself. You got publicity wherever you could, and the fact that she hadn't yet signed Dex—and probably never would—was no one's business but her own.

Hans had almost clicked his heels with respect.

"I suppose it sounds silly," she'd said in a way that made it clear she didn't think it silly at all, "but the car's my lucky charm. The repairs will have to wait until we're done shooting."

Hans, who'd dealt with Hollywood's finest for years, knew they were as superstitious as his Gypsy forebears. Still, he'd permitted himself an upraised eyebrow.

"Of course, Miss Palmer. But you understand that the car will not work dependably until repairs are made?"

"Certainly," Eve had said and driven off jauntily, as if she'd always longed to pilot a motorized sauna.

Now here she sat, the AC barely wheezing, the windows only willing to open an inch, the engine giving an ominous shudder every few minutes. Her hair was damp, her silk suit was plastered to her skin—and that wasn't the worst of it.

This was the last day of filming *The Ghost Stallion,* the hideous movie she'd inherited from her predecessor. She ought to be out on location, making certain nothing else went wrong. Instead, she was going to be trapped in her office while Zachary Landon, Charles's son, peered into cabinets, counted paper clips and tsk-tsked over every dime she'd spent.

It had been shock enough to learn of Charles's death, but to find out that his son was flying in to check up on her . . .

His accountant son, the one Charles had mentioned when Eve had tried to explain how East Coast bankers had almost destroyed Triad. She hadn't been sure a man like Charles would understand, but he had.

"Some money men have no imagination at all," he'd said.

Eve had sighed with relief. "Exactly. Filmmaking is a unique business, Mr. Landon. Mr. Tolland tried explaining that to the bank's accountants, but——"

"Call me Charles, please. Yes, I can imagine what you went through with the bean counters. Hell, when I think that my own son is one of them . . ."

"An accountant?"

"Zachary," Charles had said, his face darkening, "in with a bunch of effete Boston jackasses instead of taking his rightful place at my side. It's enough to send my blood pressure through the top of the tube."

Which was pretty much what it was doing to hers now, Eve thought as she edged the car forward.

Charles had understood instinctively that it would take time, money and a few breathtaking risks to save Triad. His accountant son would not.

"Damn," she said, and gave the steering wheel a sharp whack with her fist.

Traffic began moving and Eve slipped the car into gear and urged it forward. Somehow, she'd have to *make* him understand. If only she could get to the office before he began poking his ink-smudged fingertips into things.

The cellular phone in the console rang. Eve snatched it up.

It was her secretary. Eve listened, the expression on her face going from concern to dismay to despair. "Are you sure, Emma? Must I really go out there?"

Yes. She must. Eve grimaced, snapped out a few orders and slammed down the phone.

There was a problem on the set again, a disagreement between the movie's egotistical male lead and Francis Cranshaw, its equally asinine director. She had no choice but to deal with it before she dealt with Zachary Landon.

Men, she thought in disgust, men and their damned arrogance.

An opening suddenly appeared in the next lane. Eve accelerated hard and swung into it, cutting off a black Porsche that was trying to do the same thing. The Porsche's brakes squealed as she shot past it.

Eve glanced into her mirror as the Porsche's horn gave a long, angry blast. She could see nothing of the other driver except mirrored sunglasses above a thinned, angry mouth and an aggressive jaw.

He said something—yelled it, probably. Eve didn't have to hear the words to know they were not pleasant.

Too bad, she thought. With a little smile of grim pleasure, she stepped down on the gas and left the Porsche and its driver engulfed in a cloud of black smoke.

Zach let out a string of words that should have turned the air blue. It had been a woman driving the silver Jaguar—he'd just had time to see the bright gold hair before she'd left him eating dust.

His fingers tightened on the steering wheel of the Porsche. For one wild moment, he fantasized about speeding up, forcing the silver car onto the shoulder of the road, hauling out the driver and...

And what? Slugging women wasn't his style, not even women like the one he'd spent the flight out here reading about.

Eve Palmer, he thought, and a muscle knotted in his jaw.

He sighed and loosened his white-knuckled grip on the steering wheel. This was not shaping up as a good day. Everything that could go wrong had, from the minute he'd hit the Denver airport. His plane had been late getting off the ground, the ride had been bumpy, and the much-touted in-flight telephone had worked only after the flight engineer had put in an appearance with a screwdriver and a roll of duct tape.

But the phone had worked then, well enough to bring Zach the information he'd needed to fill in the holes in the Triad file. What he'd learned had not made him happy.

Triad's costs were up, its profits down, and it was easy to see why. His first guess had been right. The CEO, Eve Palmer, was about as qualified to head the company as she was to perform brain surgery.

"A woman CEO?" Cade had said, in the couple of minutes they'd had to compare notes this morning. His brother had grinned. "Yeah, I've got one to deal with in Dallas, too. When will these broads admit they don't belong in business?"

Zach didn't think that way. Women drivers were one thing, but he had no problem with women in the boardroom—if their ability was what had got them there.

And that was the problem. Eve Palmer had not climbed the corporate ladder, she'd scaled it on her back in a tangle of silken sheets. It was a mixed metaphor, but how else could you describe a woman who'd won her spot at Triad by becoming Charles Landon's lover?

The facts were indisputable, starting with the file itself and some notes in his father's hand.

"The Palmer woman is beautiful," Charles had written. "Clever, and more than ambitious."

Zach snorted. Calling her ambitious was understating it. The woman was twenty-five years old. She'd shown up in Hollywood in her teens, apparently from nowhere. Like a million other girls with a million other dreams, she'd been determined to become an actress. But she hadn't figured on the endless supply of other Eves and Kims and Winonas who arrived on almost every bus.

Undeterred, she had taken other jobs.

She'd modeled. She'd waitressed. She'd sold panty hose and makeup. She'd been a secretary in an office and learned word processing, and in between, she'd even managed to land walk-ons in a couple of movies Zach had never heard of.

Then she'd lucked out. A temporary job as secretary to Howard Tolland, Triad's former owner, had blossomed into a full-time position. And then Charles Landon had come along.

Zach's mouth twisted. The rest, as they said, was history.

Whether she'd warmed the old man's bed before or after he handed her Triad was unclear, but it didn't matter. The file said it all. Charles had met her one day, taken her out that night. A week later, he'd moved her into the executive office.

Traffic was thinning. Zach shifted gears and let the Porsche build up some speed. Eve Palmer had to have a really special talent to have been able to play the old man for a sucker.

Maybe it ran in the family, he thought with a tight smile as he turned onto the exit ramp. Hell, he'd been taken in by a woman, too, one who didn't care a damn about simple things like common decency and morality.

Not that it was anything personal. He was here to pull Triad back from the brink, make it an acceptable if not attractive part of the Landon package . . . but hey, if that meant that Eve Palmer ended up a casualty, who could blame him for taking some small pleasure from it?

All he had to do now was find Triad's office. He frowned at the numbers on the vaguely run-down buildings that lined Sepulveda Boulevard. It had to be here somewhere.

There it was on the corner, a boxy cement building in a shade of pink so ugly it made his teeth ache.

Zach swung the Porsche into the parking area and shut off the engine. Then he stepped out onto the asphalt, grabbed his tweed jacket from the seat and headed briskly toward the front door.

Moments later, he was out in the parking lot again, frowning darkly. He'd made a point of telephoning ahead so that the Palmer woman would be waiting for him in her office. But she wasn't. She was, her flustered secretary had said, out on location with the director, Francis Cranshaw.

"A problem came up on the set, Mr. Landon, and Miss Palmer had to go out there. She asked if you'd please make yourself comfortable and wait."

Wait? Zach's jaw tightened as he strode toward the Porsche. The hell he would wait. A problem on the set. Did she really expect him to believe that? Eve Palmer was either trying to avoid him or trying to bring him to heel, but he'd be damned if he'd let her do either.

It had been a job, prying directions to the set from her secretary.

"It's a pretty remote area," she'd said.

"I assure you," Zach had said with what he'd hoped was a polite smile, "I'll find it."

He climbed into the Porsche, yanked on his mirrored sunglasses and stabbed the key into the ignition.

"Remote location, hell," he muttered, and shot from the parking lot.

An hour later, Zach was driving down what no one in his right mind would have called a road, cursing under his breath and wondering if the secretary hadn't deliberately sent him on a wild-goose chase.

What kind of film would anyone shoot in a place like this? For the past twenty minutes, there'd been nothing on the horizon but cactus, scrubby things he thought were trees and tumbles of reddish rock. He had not seen a car or a living soul, unless you counted a scrawny coyote that had trotted past without so much as a glance.

The Porsche whined in protest as Zach drove it across what looked to be a dry streambed lined with small rocks. If the secretary hadn't deliberately misled him, he thought grimly, then Eve Palmer was even more incompetent than he'd imagined. She had to be, she and her director, Frances Whatsis. Both women would be nuts to shoot a picture in the middle of——

"Damn!"

Zach stood on the brakes as a galloping white horse and its rider suddenly materialized before him. The car skidded wildly, careered across the dusty track, lurched through a stand of prickly pear and came to a sickening stop inches from a pile of huge boulders. The engine coughed, coughed again and faded to silence.

After what seemed an eternity, Zach reached out and switched off the ignition. He took off his mirrored glasses, dropped them on the dashboard, undid his seat belt and only then remembered to breathe.

The white horse was gone, racing across the barren hilltop toward the far horizon. The horse's rider was rising slowly to his knees in the dirt.

Zach muttered, rose in his seat and vaulted from the car.

"Hell, man," he said as he hurried toward the fallen rider, "are you okay?"

"Yeah," the rider said, after a minute, "yeah, I'm okay. You?"

Zach laughed, but it sounded more like a croak. "Except for a pair of wobbly legs, I'm fine."

The rider stared after the cloud of dust, all that was now visible of the galloping horse.

"Guess he's gone," he said unhappily.

"Sorry about that. I didn't see you until the last minute, and——"

"What do you mean, you didn't see?"

Zach turned around. A small crowd of people was rushing toward him, headed by a little man with a goatee and a pencil-thin mustache.

"You would have to blind not to have seen Horace!"

"Look, pal, I already said I was sorry. It isn't my fault that——"

"What's going on here?"

A woman was pushing her way through the crowd. Zach thought she was a woman, at any rate. It was hard to tell. She had on a wide-brimmed hat that covered her hair and most of her face, a dusty, oversize khaki shirt and a pair of shapeless jeans. The only thing about her that was clearly visible was her anger.

"Well?" The woman brushed past the little guy with the goatee, slapped her hands on her hips and glared at Zach from under the brim of her hat. "What's going on here?"

Zach looked past her. He could see cameras now, and mike booms, and lots of other equipment he couldn't identify. If nothing else, he thought with relief, he'd found the Triad set. His gaze returned to the shapeless female standing before him. Yes. He'd found the set, and Frances Cranshaw.

"There's been a minor accident," Zach said pleasantly, "nothing to get excited about, I assure you."

"Are you all right, Pete?" the woman said, swinging toward the horseless rider.

"Yup, I'm fine."

"Was the horse injured?"

"Nah. He jest took off, is all."

"You see?" Zach said. "No harm's been done."

No harm's been done, Eve thought, glaring at the intruder from under the brim of her borrowed hat. What a stupid thing to say! Francis had reshot this same scene four times now, wasting heaven only knew how much film, and each time it had ended the same way, with him stroking that ridiculous little goatee and shaking his head and saying that it still wasn't quite what he wanted.

The only thing Eve wanted was to put the scene in the can, strip off the jeans and shirt and hat the props man had pieced together for her so the sun and the dust wouldn't finish her off permanently, jump in her car and speed to town to deal with Zachary Landon, who must have arrived by now. She'd been trying and trying to contact the office by cellular phone, but this damned place was so far off the beaten track that the fool thing wouldn't work.

And now, just when it had looked as if Pete and Horace the Wonder Horse were about to ride into posterity, this—this jerk had come along and ruined it all.

"Well," Zach said, smiling politely, "if you don't mind "

"Do you have any idea what a mess you've caused?"

Zach's smile tilted. "Madam, in case you hadn't noticed, I almost broke my neck a few minutes ago. If I were you——"

"You came barreling smack into the middle of my set, scared off my horse, injured my rider——"

"He just told you himself, he's not injured."

"And you have the nerve to stand there and tell me that no harm's been done?"

Zach's smile faded completely. "Listen, lady——"

"Don't 'listen, lady' me!" Eve snatched the hat from her head and slapped it against her leg. Her hair tumbled to her shoulders in a golden cloud. "Why didn't you slow down as you approached?"

"Approached what?" Zach said, trying not to stare at the wild mane of sunflower-bright curls, as incongruous on this ranting, shapeless creature as a garland of roses would be on a bull. Although, now that he considered, she really wasn't shapeless. He could see the high thrust of her breasts even under that boxy shirt, and there was the suggestion of a narrow waist, gently rounded hips, and long legs hidden under those jeans...

"Approached my set, that's what!"

"Look, I didn't see a thing except dirt and cactus until your horse damned near killed me."

"Horace couldn't kill anybody! He can't even find his way out of a stall without help!"

"Horace? The horse is named Horace?"

"Yes," Eve snapped, "Horace the Wonder Horse." Her face colored as Zach's brows rose. "It's not funny! That horse is worth a fortune. Why, without him——"

"Let me get this straight," Zach said slowly. "You're making a movie about a horse named Horace?"

Eve felt her face, already hot from an hour on this hillside, turn hotter. She knew how it sounded. Dammit, she felt the same way herself. It was incredible to think that Triad was wasting time on a film like this, but it hadn't been her idea. Howard Tolland had signed the contracts, made the commitments and stuck her with it.

"A movie," the man said, and laughed, "a movie about a horse named Horace."

Eve's gaze shot to his. "Okay," she said coldly, "you've had your laugh. Now turn that car around and get out of here."

"I'm afraid it's not that simple," Zach said, his eyes narrowing.

"It's you that's simple, mister. This is a closed set on private property, and you have no right to be here. I'm telling you again. Turn around and get out of here."

"Trust me, lady." Zach looked past Frances Cranshaw, trying to identify Eve Palmer in the sea of interested faces watching them. "You don't want to toss me off this set."

Terrific, Eve thought, just what she needed. Another out-of-work actor invading the set. They did it all the time. The UPS guy was an actor, and the kid from Western Union, and even the pizza delivery girl, all of them determined to make an impression.

Well, this man had certainly done that, but who could blame him for trying? She sighed and slapped her hat against her leg.

"Look," she said, not unkindly, "why don't you leave your press book with——"

"My what?"

"Your photos. Your résumé, whatever. If a part comes up, we'll get in touch."

"A part? You think I'm after a part in your two-bit horse opera? You actually think that I..." Zach clamped his lips together. Why was he letting this woman, this Frances Cranshaw, irritate him so? His eyes narrowed. And where was Eve Palmer? Was she such a bitch that she was going to let her director take the rap for what was a CEO's responsibility? He folded his arms over his chest. "I'm not going to waste my time with you, lady. Where's your boss?"

Eve's brows rose. "My what?"

"Come on, don't play dumb. Where is she?"

"Okay," she said, "that's it. You have two minutes to get out of here."

"Really," he said, his voice a smooth purr of amusement.

"Look, don't push your luck. You interrupted my shoot, ran off my horse——"

"Your star, you mean." He smirked. "Horace, the Wonder Horse."

"Laugh if you like. But if we can't find Horace..."

Eve's words came to an abrupt halt. What if they couldn't? What if the damned horse was gone for good? A chill settled in the pit of her stomach. Could Francis finish the film anyway? She already knew the answer, knew what would happen to Triad.

"Frankly," the man said, his smirk deepening, "I think old Horace is probably in Mexico by now."

Eve felt her mouth begin to tremble. "I bet you think this is pretty damned funny."

"What I think, madam, is that I've stumbled into the middle of a fiasco."

She stepped forward, her face turned up to his. "You're the fiasco," she said, her voice trembling along with her lips. "If we don't find that damned horse—if we don't find him..."

All her bravado seemed to vanish. Zach frowned. Tears were rising in those blue eyes, turning them the color of sapphires.

"Oh, hell," he said. "Dammit, don't cry!"

"I'm not crying," Eve said fiercely. "I never——"

But she was. Zach muttered a short, sharp word under his breath and did the only thing he could.

He reached out, drew her into his arms and kissed her.

CHAPTER THREE

LATER, when he tried to make sense out of his own behavior, Zach would tell himself his brain must have gone on a holiday. Otherwise, why would he have taken this ill-tempered, sharp-tongued, dust-begrimed vixen in his arms?

Not that his brain had shut down altogether. If anything, it was working overtime, delivering enough sensory messages to put him on overload.

He heard the crowd's shocked gasp, heard the smothered exclamation of the woman just as his mouth found hers, then felt her stunned resistance, followed quickly by her indignant struggles. He was even aware of the amused tut-tut of a little voice inside his head as it asked him just what, exactly, he thought he was doing.

The problem was that the voice asked the question a fraction of a second too late. By then, Zach's mouth had closed over Frances Cranshaw's mouth. And the little voice faded to a whisper.

She tasted sweet, like the nectar of a flower. And cool, like a swift-running mountain stream. But mostly—mostly, she tasted like a meal for a starving man, and he had the sudden crazy thought he'd been hungry all his life.

Until now.

Heat coiled in his belly, then shot through his blood. His arms tightened around her.

Stop it, the voice insisted. *Let her go. She doesn't want this—see how she's fighting you? And you don't want it either. You don't know this dame, you don't like her, and you're sure as hell not the kind of man who goes around forcing women.*

But he didn't let her go. He drew her closer, bent her over his arm, one hand slipping up to cup the back of her head, his fingers twining in the silken spill of her golden hair while his mouth moved against hers, offering, asking...

A soft, keening sound rose in her throat. It was a sound Zach had heard before. He knew what it meant, understood it, and it made the blood roar in his ears.

"Yes," he whispered against her lips, and all at once her hands were curled into his shirt and she went from fighting him to hot, sweet acquiescence.

He felt her body soften, her head droop against his arm. He heard her breath catch as she made that whisper of surrender again.

And then someone in the crowd laughed.

"Way to go, Evie," a male voice called.

And that was when Zach knew that the woman in his arms wasn't Frances Cranshaw at all.

She was Eve Palmer.

The realization stunned him, and his hold on her loosened. Eve reacted instantly, stumbling backward as she shoved free of his arms and then slapping him, hard, across the face.

"You bastard!"

Slowly, Zach lifted his hand to his cheek. Eve Palmer's eyes blazed, her lips trembled. She was a study in feminine outrage, and he might have been impressed—

if he hadn't felt her incredible response in his arms, just seconds ago.

No, Zach thought, hell, no. He wasn't going to let her get away with this.

"Nice," he said in a low voice, "very nice. But names and games don't work with me, baby. You're wasting your time."

She pointed a shaking finger toward the Porsche. "You have one minute to get into your car and drive out of here. Otherwise——"

"I wouldn't give ultimatums, if I were you."

"So help me, mister, I'll call the police. You can't walk onto my set and—and tyrannize me!"

"Tyrannize you?" Zach laughed sharply and folded his arms over his chest. "Is that what you'll charge me with? Tyranny?"

"How about sexual assault? Does that sound better?"

"Come on, baby, give me a break. Who're you kidding? You were all over me, breathing hot and heavy." He caught her by the wrist as her hand arced toward him again. "Don't do it," he said grimly, "or I'll call the cops myself."

Eve glared at him. What a despicable SOB he was! This town was a paradise for good-looking, walking, talking egos but this one was in a class by himself. Kissing her was bad enough, but to have the audacity to claim she'd enjoyed it...

She'd despised everything about that kiss, from the feel of his arms to the taste of his mouth to the scent of him as he'd held her and if, just for an instant, she'd seemed to—to relax in his embrace, it had only been because he'd caught her so off guard, because she had never expected him to do anything so boorish and coarse...

... because she'd never expected his lips to brush hers with fire, his body to saturate hers with heat...

The ridiculous thought horrified her as much as his sudden laughter. It was as if he'd read her mind.

Color raced into her cheeks. Eve wrenched her hand from his, spun on her heel and pushed her way through the crowd, determinedly ignoring the whispers and the smiles. The rusty trailer that served as Triad's on-location office loomed ahead, looking more like a sanctuary than the hotbox it was, and she headed straight for it.

He caught up to her when she was halfway there, his hand falling like a steel bar across her shoulder.

"I don't like to be ignored, Miss Palmer."

"No," Eve said as he swung her toward him. "No, I can see that. Obviously, you'd rather be arrested."

"We need to talk," he said through his teeth.

"We *have* talked. I offered you a choice and you decided you'd rather spend the night in jail than get off this set."

"Spare me the melodrama, please." Zach looked past her at the trailer that stood baking in the sun. "Is that your office?"

"Francis?" Eve rose on her toes and glared over Zach's shoulder. "Francis, call the police!"

The little man with the mustache and the goatee came rushing up, wringing his hands.

"I will, if you insist," he said in a stage whisper. "But the negative publicity will——"

"Of course," Zach muttered. "Francis, with an *i*, not an *e*."

The little man drew himself up. "That is correct, sir. I am Francis Cranshaw, the famous director. And you are...?"

"Francis, dammit," Eve said furiously, "will you stop being so polite? This isn't a time for introductions!" She glared at Zach. "I don't care who he is. I want him out of here, now!"

Zach smiled coldly. "Ah, but you should, Miss Palmer. Care for introductions, I mean."

"Listen here, mister, as far as I'm concerned——"

"As far as you're concerned, the ride is over." Zach paused, wanting to draw out the pleasure of the moment, and that was when he saw the first horrified glint of comprehension edge into her eyes. "That's right," he said softly, and he smiled. "Evie, love, let me introduce myself. My name is Zachary Landon."

A couple of hours later, Zach was pacing the faded carpet in the Triad office reception area. His trousers were torn, his tweed jacket was covered with dust, and his mood more than matched his appearance.

This morning's sweet moment of victory had faded and had been replaced by his irritation at the childish power game Eve Palmer was playing. He'd been out here fifteen minutes now, cooling his heels, while she undoubtedly sat behind her desk and deliberately let the minutes tick away.

He reached the edge of the carpet, turned and paced in the other direction. It was just too bad she'd made it to town before he had, but then, she hadn't had to waste precious minutes shoving the Porsche back on the road or coaxing it into starting up again. He'd still been under the Porsche's hood when an all-too-familiar silver Jaguar had shot past him.

"No," Zach had muttered as he stared after it, "no..."

When he'd finally arrived at the Triad office, the Jaguar had been parked in the lot, secure in its silver insolence. Zach had stared at it, ground his teeth together and wondered why he'd been stupid enough to laugh early this morning when Grant had offered to trade.

He could be in New York right now, buying a chocolate malted for some twelve-year-old kid instead of wondering how high a man's blood pressure could get, all thanks to one woman.

"Dammit," he said under his breath.

"Sir?"

He turned and glowered at Eve's secretary. The woman smiled nervously, the way she would if she was facing a certified lunatic.

"Did you—did you say something, Mr. Landon?"

Zach's eyes narrowed. "I said that I'm tired of pacing the floor."

She shot to her feet as he strode past her.

"Mr. Landon! Sir, Miss Palmer isn't ready to see you just yet. You can't——"

"Watch me."

Eve was standing in the tiny private bathroom that connected to her office. She'd showered away the grime, changed from the overalls to an ivory silk dress she kept in her office closet for emergencies, and now she was trying to figure out how to best recoup her losses.

An apology seemed the only solution.

Her mouth curved down. What she wanted to do was stalk outside, walk up to Zachary Landon and slug him again. But common sense told her not to do it. His behavior had been rude and awful, but then, hers hadn't been so terrific, either. That was what she'd decided to tell him, and if he had half a brain, he'd agree.

She shouldn't have gotten so angry at him for barreling into the unmarked set. As for Zachary Landon—for all she knew, he made a habit of kissing women he'd never met before. The bottom line was that she should have controlled her temper, and he should have acted with more decorum. It was, as far as she could see, a draw. Surely, he would see that, too....

The door slammed against the wall as it was flung open. Eve spun around, her hand to her throat. Zachary Landon stood in the doorway, covered with dust and grime and looking as if he was on the verge of exploding. Emma peered past his shoulder, her face white.

"Miss Palmer," she said, "Eve, I'm sorry. I told Mr. Landon he had to wait, but——"

"But he got tired of it," Zach said, with a chilly smile. "So he decided to take matters into his own hands."

Eve took a deep breath, shut off the bathroom light and walked toward him.

"So I see." She looked at her secretary. "It's all right. You can go."

Emma nodded. "I'll be just outside," she said, shooting Zach a warning glance.

The door swung shut. Eve waited, counted to ten, then forced a smile to her lips.

"Won't you sit down, Mr. Landon?"

The woman was cool as a cucumber, Zach thought as he looked at her. The grubby overalls were gone, as was the dust, and she'd pulled that wild mane of golden hair back from her face. It was a style that would have looked matronly on most women, but the severe lines only emphasized the size and color of her eyes and the clean, sculpted bones that lay just beneath her creamy skin.

"I'll stand, thanks."

Eve nodded. "As you wish."

She walked to her desk but didn't sit down behind it. That would put him at too much of an advantage. Instead, she took a deep breath and said what had to be said.

"I'm sorry we got off to such a poor start this morning, Mr. Landon."

Zach's brows lifted. "Was that what it was, Miss Palmer?" His tone was smooth as silk. "I wasn't quite sure how to describe it."

To his immense satisfaction, color stained her high cheekbones.

"Mr. Landon——"

"Please." Zach smiled. "I hardly think there's any reason for us to stand on formality, do you? Considering the intimacy of our relationship, I mean."

Eve's eyes narrowed. "Look, I'm willing to forget what happened, but if you insist on bringing it up——"

"I was referring to our business status, Eve," he said pleasantly. "After all, you're Triad's CEO and I'm its new owner."

Her eyes flew to his. "Of course. I thought..." She cleared her throat. "You're right, Zach. I, ah, I hoped you'd see it that way."

His smile was open and easy. "What way?"

"Well, there's no sense in us being enemies, is there? I mean, we both have Triad's best interests at heart. So if we put aside what happened earlier——"

"Sorry, Eve, I'm not sure I'm following you."

His expression was innocent, but that didn't fool her for a minute. He was up to something, she knew it. But what?

She tried to smile. "I'm talking about the—the incident on the set."

His shoulder brushed hers as he strolled past her. He moved slowly around the office, pausing now and then to look at the old black and white still photos hanging on the walls.

"Your collection?" he asked, gazing at a shot of an intense Humphrey Bogart and a languid Ingrid Bergman.

Eve nodded. "Yes. I've always been a fan of old movies." She waited for him to say something but he didn't. She cleared her throat. "What about you?"

He looked at her and smiled, but she could see that the smile was false, touching his lips but not his eyes.

A knot of anger formed in her belly. Did he think this was easy for her? What she'd told him was the truth, they had gotten off to a bad start, and even though ninety-nine percent of the fault was his, she was willing to shoulder half the blame—but she'd be damned if she was going to crawl.

"Old movies seem so unrealistic."

She blinked and looked at him. He was walking slowly toward her, that phony half-smile curling across his handsome face. Her breath caught. Surely, he wasn't going to try to kiss her again. If he did... If he did, she'd slap him so hard both his ears would be on the same side of his head.

"Unrealistic?" she repeated with an uneasy smile. Why didn't he stand still? And what did he care what kind of movies she liked?

He smiled, reached out and brushed a stray strand of hair from her cheek so quickly that the only proof he'd done it was the jolt of electricity his fingers left behind.

"Yes. I always find myself watching the actors and thinking that they're overdoing it. You follow?"

"No," Eve said. Her voice sounded thready and she frowned and spoke again. "No," she said, more strongly, "I'm afraid I..." She went silent as he strolled behind her desk and ran his hand over the back of her chair. "I'm afraid I don't."

"Sure you do. There's even a phrase for it. Chewing up the scenery, isn't that it?" Zach smiled as he sat down behind the desk. "You know what I mean, Eve."

Eve stared at him. He tilted back the chair, looped his hands behind his head and put his feet up on the desk. *Her* desk, she thought, gritting her teeth. Her desk, her chair, her office...

"I'm much more impressed by the current crop of actors."

Her eyes flew to his face. "Mr. Landon," she said with a stiff smile, "Zach, if you don't mind——"

"They've got these nice, natural techniques. You watch somebody like, I don't know, Jack Nicholson, you think there's a guy you could deal with. When he's playing a part, you never think that he is. He makes it seem real."

"This is fascinating, Zach, but——"

"But?"

"But we both know that you came here to see Triad's books." She reached for the phone. "I'll tell Emma to——"

Zach's hand closed on her wrist. "I suppose I did get carried away with all this talk about acting." He let go of her and smiled tightly as he rose to his feet.

"Yes. Well, as I said, I'm sure your views on the subject are fascinating, but——"

"Come on, Eve. You don't think that at all."

Their eyes met, and what she saw in the sea-green depths of his made it difficult to swallow.

"I know you won't believe this," she said carefully, "but I'm trying my best to be polite."

"Believe it or not, I'm trying my best to be polite, too." A muscle knotted high in his jaw. "Hell, if I wasn't, I'd already have told you that you're wasting your talents on the production end of things." Zach came slowly toward her. "That's what made me think about acting, and how some people make it seem so real."

Eve swallowed hard. She didn't want to step back; she knew instinctively that giving ground would be a mistake, but he was too close, so close that she could see the little laugh lines around his eyes.

Not that he was laughing now. On the contrary. She had never seen a man's face look so hard.

"Perhaps you'd like to tell me what it is you're talking about, Zach."

He laughed softly. "I'm talking about acting, Evie. I told you that. I'm talking about you, in particular."

"Me?" She took that step she hadn't wanted to take, but it was an error. She knew that as soon as her shoulders hit the wall.

"You, Evie. Why, you're the best actress I've ever seen."

"I don't find any of this amusing, Zach. I thought you wanted to talk about Triad."

"I do." He smiled. "I am. I'm assessing your award-winning performance. The ease with which you switch from role to role amazes me. Spitfire one minute, seductress the next, coolheaded executive when the need arises..."

"Goodbye, Mr. Landon," Eve said coldly. "If and when you decide to discuss business, telephone my secretary and we'll set up an appointment."

Zach's hands shot out as she started to step forward. His palms hit the wall on either side of her, caging her between his outstretched arms.

"I'm talking it right now." His words were clipped, and all the smiling pretense was gone. "What's the problem? Did you expect me to buy into the efficient lady-exec act the same way I bought into the others?"

"So much for civility," Eve said, her voice shaking a little. "And so much for your father's assessment of you."

"My father talked to you about me?"

"He said you were a human calculator, but he was wrong. What you are is a fat, swollen ego."

Zach's lips drew back from his teeth. "Is that right?"

"You're angry about what happened this morning and you're taking it out on me."

"Dear, sweet Evie. You're a woman of many talents, but as a shrink you're an absolute failure."

Eve glared at him. "My name isn't Evie. And who do you think you are, talking to me like this? King of the universe?"

Zach grinned. "That's not a bad analogy, Evie. I *am* king—king of your world, anyway. I'm the boss and you're the peon. Or hadn't you noticed?"

"I am head of this company."

"You were, until two minutes ago."

He could see that his words had taken her by surprise. It showed in her sudden pallor, in the way her breath hitched, but he had to give her credit. She kept looking straight at him, and there wasn't even a hint of the weeping routine she'd pulled earlier.

"I see," she said. "Just like that."

Zach's hands fell to his sides. He shrugged. "What did you expect? A formal letter of dismissal? You're out, Eve. Just like that."

She didn't want to beg. God, no, she wouldn't do that. But he owed her an explanation, he owed her more than this....

"If you'd just give me a chance to try and make you understand why we've been losing money..."

"No."

"Because there are reasons, you see. Your father——"

"My father was a fool," Zach said sharply. "Unfortunately for you, it's not a trait that runs in the family."

"Look, I know you had a—a bad morning, but it isn't fair to blame it on me. And that's what you're doing, I know you are——"

"Trust me, Eve. I planned on dumping you from the second I landed in L.A. What happened after that didn't change a thing."

"I embarrassed you in front of those people, and——"

"By slapping me, you mean?" Zach gave a little laugh. "Maybe you've forgotten that by the time you got around to hitting me, that bunch of weirdos had already seen you melt like butter in my arms."

"That's absurd. I didn't melt. And they're not weirdos, they're technicians and actors." Eve stabbed her hands onto her hips. "But you wouldn't know about that. You don't know much about anything except numbers.''

He could see the fury raging in her now. Her cheeks were crimson with color, and her eyes snapped like the darkest, bluest sapphires. Zach felt a swift rush of pleasure at the sight. She hadn't embarrassed him out on that hillside, but she sure as hell had made him feel like a damned fool, and it was a delight to turn the tables now and watch her squirm.

It was just that it would have been better if she'd look like she was squirming. If she'd ground her teeth, or snarled. If she'd turned blotchy under her makeup...

But she wasn't doing any of that. In fact, she still looked like the most gorgeous creature he'd ever seen.

No wonder the old man had been so easy.

"You're right," Zach said coldly. "I don't know a rat's whisker about movies. As for numbers—anybody with an adding machine would have a heart attack once he ran the figures in your files."

"But you haven't seen my files." Eve gestured to the cabinets that lined the walls. "If you'd just take a look and let me explain——"

"You're wasting your time, Eve. I have a full report on Triad." He smiled tightly. "The one the auditors made for my father when he bought this place. I read it from cover to cover on the flight out here."

"So what? It's obvious you don't understand it. Charles did. He saw the potential in Triad."

Zach leaned against the desk, his eyes on hers. "Tell me something," he said softly. "Do you miss him?"

"Do I...? Charles, you mean?"

His teeth showed very whitely in a quick, mirthless smile.

"Yeah. That's who I mean, Evie. Do you miss the old man at all?"

"I don't see what that has to do with anything."

"Humor me." His teeth flashed again in that same smile, one that sent a whisper of warning along her spine. "Do you at least think of him once in a while?"

"Of course. Your father was very kind to me. He didn't know much about the film business, but——"

"But he didn't have to."

"That's right, he didn't. He was willing to learn."

"Yeah, I'll bet." Zach leaned away from the desk and moved toward her. "And I'll bet you were one hell of a teacher."

"I taught him what I could."

"What did you teach him?" Zach put his hand on her arm. Her skin was fever hot; he could feel its heat straight through her silk dress. "I'm curious."

"I taught him about Triad, about this business.... Don't do that," she said sharply, as his hand stroked down her arm. His touch was light, but it sent a tongue of flame licking through her.

"I told you before, Eve, my old man was the fool, not me." His voice thickened. "That's not all you taught him, is it?"

Eve stiffened. "I don't like what you're implying."

Zach's hands closed lightly around her face. She held herself rigid, but the pressure of his fingers was powerful. Slowly, he lifted her chin.

"What did you teach him, Eve?"

She stared at him, despising him for what he thought, despising herself for the whisper of heat his touch was sending through her blood.

"Nothing I'd be willing to teach you," she said coldly.

His gaze fell to her mouth, then lifted to her eyes.

"You already taught me something, on that hillside." He moved closer, so that only a breath separated them. "You taught me that you're good at what you do—but I keep wondering, was that your best shot?"

"So help me, I'll scream if you——"

"Scream? Because a man kisses you?" Zach laughed as his head lowered slowly to hers. "From what I've heard of Hollywood, Eve, a kiss between friends isn't anything more than an updated handshake."

"We'renotfriends,"shesaid,"we'renotevenacquaintan
"

Zach's mouth closed over hers.

Eve froze, telling herself that to fight him would only be to humiliate herself and give him the satisfaction he wanted.

I won't move, she told herself, *I won't give him the pleasure of reacting, I won't....*

She swayed as Zach shifted the angle of the kiss. His mouth moved against hers, not in hard demand but softly, coaxingly. She felt the swift, silken brush of his tongue across the seam of her lips.

I won't react, she thought desperately, *I won't....*

His teeth sank gently into her bottom lip at the same moment that his hand rose and cupped her breast. A soft sound rose in her throat, one she didn't even want to think about. To her horror, she felt her nipple rise and seek the heat of his palm.

Stop him, she thought desperately, *stop him!*

Instead, she opened her mouth to his.

His tongue thrust between her lips, filling her with his taste and with the promise of an ever greater fulfillment.

His arms swept around her, crushing her to him, and the world spun out from beneath her feet.

She heard his soft groan, heard the echo of her own breathless whisper as the kiss deepened. Nothing mattered, nothing but this. She felt the heavy race of his heart beneath her palms, the swelling power of his erection against her groin. The heat, and the hardness, made her begin to tremble, and she stumbled against the desk.

Zach came with her, his hungry mouth drinking from hers, his hands hot as he grasped her skirt and hiked it around her hips. His fingers brushed over her thighs and she made a soft, incoherent cry and flung her arms around his neck....

Suddenly, his hands closed over hers. With a muffled curse, he tore her fingers away.

Eve's eyes flew open. Zach was looking at her with such smoldering hatred in his face that it took her breath away.

Bile rose in her throat. She clapped her hand to her mouth and stumbled into the bathroom.

He was gone when she came out, but she knew that didn't mean a thing. She opened her closet, took out her briefcase and her jacket and left the office without looking back.

Emma was waiting, her eyes wide and tearstained.

"He said—he said you were leaving," she whispered, "that he'd fired you."

Somehow, Eve managed to smile. "I'll send for the rest of my things," she said, and then she hurried out the door, wondering who she despised more, Zachary Landon or herself.

CHAPTER FOUR

RAIN sheeted down across the parking area in front of the building that held the Triad offices, turning the worn asphalt into a sea of glistening ebony. Beyond, cars navigated the roadway with caution, their lights bright against the gloom of late afternoon.

Rain, Zach thought as he stood staring out the window of his office, that was all he'd seen for the past who knew how many days, nothing but endless, miserable rain. Where was all that California sunshine people were always boasting about?

The telephone buzzed. Zach reached back without looking and hit the on button.

"Yeah? What is it, Emma?"

"Mr. Kaplan of State Affiliated Bank is on line one, Mr. Landon. Will you take the call?"

Zach turned, kicked out his chair and sat down. "Tell me something, will you?"

"If I can, sir."

"Is it always this cheerful in L.A.?"

"Sir?"

"The rain, Emma. Doesn't it ever stop?"

Emma's tone was cool. "Fall is our rainy season, Mr. Landon."

"Winter's our snowy season back East, but that doesn't mean it snows every day. This isn't good for the L.A. image, Emma. Somebody should pass the word to the Chamber of Commerce."

"Did you want to dictate a letter to them, sir?" Emma said politely.

Zach sighed. He'd fired Eve Palmer and moved into her office a week ago, but her secretary still treated him as if he was a leper.

"Never mind. Just put Mr. Kaplan through, please."

Minutes later, Zach hung up the phone, tilted back his chair, linked his hands behind his head and put his feet up on his desk.

Bob Kaplan had been pleasant. He'd even invited Zach to a party—"Nothing fancy, just a barbecue somebody's giving for this guy who's being transferred—" before getting down to business.

State Affiliated could not extend the due date on Triad's loan.

"I'm sure you understand, Landon," Kaplan had said, "with your background. I got to tell you, I'd never have agreed to the loan in the first place. It was Ed Brubeck approved it, not me." Kaplan had chuckled. "Then again, maybe that's why I'm staying here, in LaLa Land, and Brubeck's been transferred to Arden."

Zach had laughed politely, but he wasn't laughing now. Kaplan was right. Zach did, indeed, understand why the loan couldn't be extended. It was bad business. And he was certain he also understood why old Ed Brubeck, whoever he was, had agreed to lend Eve the money in the first place.

He'd been dazzled by her, the same way the old man had. What man wouldn't be? Zach thought grimly, as he remembered what had happened in this very room just a week ago.

Kissing Eve had started as a game, an object lesson to show her that he knew what she was and wasn't impressed, but it had changed into something he didn't like to think about, a dark hunger to possess her that had almost driven him past the point of no return.

Scowling, he dropped his feet to the floor and brought his chair up straight. How many poor saps had she worked her black magic on? He'd spent the past week poring through Triad's files, and it was all there, the talent she had for conning men into letting her get away with dollars-and-cents murder.

There was his father. And the bank's Ed Brubeck. Even the caterer who delivered meals to the set seemed to have been on the list. The guy still brought the food, but with Eve gone, the fare had gone from roast beef to hot dogs.

"You don't pay me enough for roast beef," he'd said when Zach passed along the crew's complaints.

And what about the guy who owned the Wonder Horse? Horace had returned, minus a shoe but in good health, but his owner was protesting. Eve had convinced him, he said, to let the horse work for far less than his usual fee.

"Eve made me promises," he said, "and now she's gone."

Promises, Zach thought. Oh, yeah, he'd just bet she'd made promises!

What she hadn't done was run Triad. It was already in debt, and about to go even deeper. Eve had made commitments toward a new film, commitments Zach had just discovered.

Hell, by the time he figured a way to pull Triad out of deep water, it would be next Christmas!

He shoved back his chair, got to his feet and shrugged on his jacket. Emma looked up in surprise as he pulled open the door to his office and strode past her desk.

"Are you going out, Mr. Landon?"

"Yes," Zach snapped, "I am."

"But you have an appointment."

"Cancel it."

Zach slammed the door shut behind him, trotted down the cracked steps and headed for the Porsche.

Eve had taken a sick company and made it worse. Now Triad was in its death throes but it was dying on his watch, dammit. He'd figured on being out here a few days, maybe five, but it had been a week already and there was no end in sight. He had a life and a business back East, and he was damned if he was going to spend any more of it cleaning up a mess his father and Eve had made.

"I've had it," he growled as he stabbed the key into the Porsche's ignition.

And it was time Eve knew it.

Eve sat curled on the sofa in her living room. She was wearing her tattiest robe and sipping a cup of tea as she watched the rain come down. The miserable weather was a perfect match for her mood.

She had come home almost an hour ago, after a fruitless morning and afternoon of interviews, feeling as low as she could ever recall feeling. A long, hot bath had done nothing to improve her spirits, and neither had twenty minutes of staring blindly at Oprah on TV.

She sighed and told herself not to sit around feeling sorry for herself, but maybe that was better than the rage that had driven her the past week.

God, how she hated Zach Landon and men like him!

When you were blond, and blue-eyed, and halfway attractive, you learned early on that even if you wore sackcloth and ashes, some men figured you'd been put on this earth for only one purpose.

It was funny, really. She hadn't expected that from Charles's son. Charles had not judged her by her looks; why would his offspring? Her big worry had been that Zachary Landon would be a human cipher, too wrapped up in bottom lines and balance sheets to understand Triad's unique problems.

Eve's mouth turned down. Instead, he'd turned out to be the kind of man who'd taken a look at her, decided what she was and set out to punish her for it.

And he'd succeeded. She was out of work, and the only way to describe her prospects was to say they certainly didn't look promising.

Eve got to her feet. No, they weren't promising at all, she thought as she brought her empty teacup into the kitchen. The trade journals didn't exactly advertise openings for out-of-work heads of companies, and even if they had, no one would hire her.

"Sorry, Eve," all her contacts said when she called, "but you know how it is."

Yes, she knew. The rumor that she'd slept her way into the top job at Triad had been bad, but this was worse. She'd been fired, she was a failure. And who would hire a failure?

She wasn't even anybody's choice for typist or word processor, she thought as she rinsed her cup and put it into the dish drainer. Nobody wanted to hire a typist or a word processor whose last job had been head of a production company.

"We don't really have anything you'd be interested in," the interviewers kept saying, and Eve kept smiling like a fool because otherwise she was afraid she'd blurt out the truth, that she was interested in anything that would pay the rent.

At the beginning, when Charles had first offered her the job at Triad, he'd talked about working out a severance package. But all that had gone by the wayside when he'd become ill.

Eve switched off the kitchen light and made her way into the living room. She needed a job. Any job, and never mind its status.

It was an old Hollywood tradition, she thought with a bitter smile, taking that breathless plunge from the heights to the depths. Veronica Lake, the forties screen siren, had ended up as a manicurist. Betty Hutton had gone from burning up the screen to burning pots in the kitchen of a parish mission. She could certainly go from...

The doorbell rang. Eve frowned. Who could it be at this hour of the afternoon?

She put her eye to the spy hole. "Yes?" she said. "What do you...?"

The words caught in her throat. It was Zachary Landon.

"Open the door, Eve."

She stared through the spy hole, taking in the expensive dark blue suit, the handsome face with its cold mouth and hostile eyes, and the rage came rushing back, so all-consuming it threatened to cut off her breath.

"Go away!"

A door creaked open across the courtyard. Zach shot a look over his shoulder before turning back to Eve.

"I don't intend to stand out here all day, Eve. Let me in."

Eve laughed. The man was incredible!

"Oh, yes, Mr. Landon. Certainly, Mr. Landon. Your wish is my command, Mr. Landon."

She didn't move a muscle. Zach leaned closer.

"Open it," he said through his teeth, "or so help me, I'll break it down!"

"Mrs. Harmon will love that." Eve smiled and raised her voice just a little. The door opposite hers was fairly trembling with anticipation. "Won't you, Mrs. Harmon? It will give you an excuse to call the police, just the way they do in all those crime shows."

"What a good idea," Zach said coldly. "Perhaps we'll be lucky enough to have a reporter come along for the ride. Having your picture splashed across the papers tomorrow ought to make your life even more interesting."

Eve's smile faded. She jerked off the chain and wrenched the door open.

"Well?" she said. "What do you want?"

"I want to talk." Zach brushed past her. "But without an audience."

She frowned, but he was right. She didn't need an audience, either, she thought as she swung the door shut.

"Five minutes," she said, turning to Zach. "After that, you're out of here."

His teeth showed in a phony smile.

"Such hostility, Evie. Anyone would think you don't like me."

"You said you came to talk, and I said you had five minutes. Now you're down to four. Believe me, I've better things to do than waste my time with you."

His gaze swept over her, taking in the long flannel robe and loosely braided hair.

"Oh, I can see that," he said tonelessly. "Lounging around the house is exhausting work."

Lounging, Eve thought, remembering the endless, and unproductive, round of interviews, lounging...

"Yes," she said with a cool smile, "that's right. It's the rain. It always makes me lazy."

Zach looked at her again. She looked anything but lazy. There was an energy to her that was almost palpable. Her creamy skin was flushed, her eyes bright, and unless he missed his guess, there was nothing under that robe but woman.

The thought made his body tighten, and he turned on his heel and walked around the small living room while Eve tapped her foot.

"When you've seen enough," she said, "be sure and let me know."

He had seen enough—enough to be puzzled. He had expected...what? Velvet chaise longues and dim light? High-heeled gold mules tucked beneath a gilded chair? He wasn't really certain. But he hadn't expected this somewhat shabby assortment of furniture, the kind that looked as if it had been rescued from secondhand shops.

Then again, he thought as he turned to Eve, he hadn't expected her to look like this, either. She didn't look like a femme fatale, she looked soft and vulnerable and almost painfully beautiful, she looked like a woman a man wanted to scoop into his arms and carry off to bed...

He frowned. "I had a call from Bob Kaplan today."

"The loan officer at State Affiliated?"

He nodded. "I'd asked him to give Triad some extra time on that final loan payment, but——"

"But he wouldn't."

"Exactly. He said——"

"I'm not interested."

It wasn't true. She was desperately interested, but she'd sooner have choked than let Zach know that.

"You're not interested," Zach repeated in a flat voice.

Eve shook her head. "No."

"I'll bet that would make the poor sap who granted you that loan in the first place feel pretty stupid."

"Ed Brubeck?"

"Yeah. Thanks to you, he's been sent to the boonies. He got dumped out of the L.A. branch and into the backwoods because he was foolish enough to..." Zach glared at her. "What's so funny?"

"You," Eve gasped, "you're funny! Just listen to you!"

"Hearing me describe a man's demotion is amusing?"

"Demotion!" Eve threw back her head and laughed some more, but her laughter stopped when Zach grabbed her, hard, by the shoulders.

"How can you laugh at another man's misfortune, dammit? Have you no heart?"

Eve wrenched free of him. "Are you stupid, or are you blind? Of course, Kaplan wouldn't extend the loan deadline. Kaplan knows zilch about making movies. Besides, he's only a bank officer."

"Only a..."

"Brubeck's a vice president. And he's just been made one of the directors. That's why he's been transferred to Arden. To the main office in Arden, I might add. And, just in case you're going to sit around waiting for the ax to fall on his head because he lent me that money, don't. His promotion came through after he'd approved the Triad loan.''

It was gratifying to see the sudden wash of crimson that swept into Zach's cheeks, but the pleasure didn't last long.

"So, you managed to climb past Kaplan,'' he said. "But then, that wouldn't have been so difficult for a woman of your talents. Look at how you worked my old man.''

"I did not work Charles,'' Eve said sharply.

"No?''

"No. He heard me express some ideas and he liked them.''

"I'll just bet he liked your ideas,'' Zach said with a taut smile. "What man wouldn't?''

Eve opened her mouth, then shut it. She'd be damned if she was going to let Zach Landon force her onto the defensive. You only lost ground, arguing with the Zach Landons of this world.

"Instead of making speeches about my morality,'' she said, her tone icy, "you might try phoning the State Affiliated office in Arden and talking with Ed Brubeck. Tell him the film's almost completed—Horace did turn up, didn't he?''

Zach nodded. "Yes,'' he said wryly, "the star returneth.''

"Good. Then you can assure Brubeck that the movie will hit the video stores within the month, and——''

"The video stores?'' Zach stared at her in disbelief. "Let me get this straight. Triad's gone into debt to make a movie that won't play in the theaters?''

"Right.''

"Dammit, woman, how could you be such a fool? What's the logic in making a movie that won't earn any money?"

"Do yourself a favor, Zach. Get your hands on some books about making movies in the nineties and read them. Maybe, with luck, you'll learn something."

The flush rose in his cheeks again. "What's that supposed to mean?"

"Lots of films go straight into video stores. They'd never recover a dime otherwise."

"Dogs, you mean."

"You're catching on."

"If this movie's so bad, why are you making it?"

Eve sighed as she walked into the kitchen.

"I inherited it," she said as she filled the kettle with water. "From the former head of the company. Any other clever questions?"

He hesitated. Everything had seemed so obvious a little while ago. But now—now, he wasn't so sure.

"Well?" She put the kettle on the burner, turned on the flame and swung toward him. "Last chance, Zach. If you've other things to ask me, ask them now."

"Horace's owner is complaining," he said brusquely, his eyes on her face. "He says he let you have the horse at a ridiculous rate."

Eve snorted, yanked open a cupboard door and began banging cups and saucers onto the counter.

"Did he bother telling you that this Horace isn't the real one? Horace went to horse heaven the week before we started filming. According to Triad's contract, I could have walked away."

"Why didn't you?"

"Because," she said patiently, "we'd already laid out big bucks for everything else. And Horace's owner offered a solution. He had another horse. It looks like Horace, but it's not as smart."

"Yeah," Zach said with a little laugh, "tell me about it."

"Do you take milk or sugar?"

"What?"

"With your tea. Milk? Or sugar?"

He didn't take tea at all, not since he was ten years old and sick with the flu and Stella had fed him endless pots of the stuff. But there was something about this tenuous peace, about standing in the warm, cramped kitchen with Eve in her flannel robe...

"Sugar," he said, frowning. "Sugar's fine."

"So? What else do you need to ask me?"

He looked at her. Her expression was bland but he knew she was enjoying this. It wasn't just that she was getting a kick out of his needing her help, although he wasn't kidding himself; she was definitely lapping it up.

But there was more to it. She was knowledgeable about moviemaking, he had to admit that, more than he'd expected and surely more knowledgeable than he. It made sense that she would be. She'd been on the fringes of the business for a long time, and once the old man had handed Triad to her, she'd probably done some fast and furious homework so that she could make herself seem indispensable. The last thing she'd have wanted would have been for Charles to have taken away her toy.

She was, after all, not just beautiful but bright.

"No more questions?"

Zach looked at her. "The caterer," he said. "The crew's not happy with his meals lately. They want roast beef. He wants more money." He paused deliberately. "Or is it just that he misses you, Eve?"

Color swept into her cheeks but her eyes never left his.

"The caterer's planning on branching into residential work," she said stiffly. "I told him that if he fed the crew well, I'd put in a word with a friend who writes an influential food column. Any other questions, Mr. Landon?"

Zach took a long drink of his tea, then put the cup down. What the hell, he thought, and he took a deep breath.

"Perhaps I was hasty in firing you," he said.

Eve grasped the edge of the counter for support. "What did you say?"

"You heard me the first time." He smiled. It was not a particularly pleasant smile, she thought giddily, but it was a smile, nonetheless. "Don't push your luck by making me repeat it."

Her hand began to shake; she set her cup down carefully on its saucer and drew a deep breath.

"Well," she said, "well."

"You do know something about the film business."

"Yes. I do. I tried to tell you that."

"Not nearly enough to rate the top spot, of course...."

The smile that was hovering on Eve's lips disappeared. "Your father disagreed."

"My father was influenced by your other assets."

Her eyes flashed. "Are we back to that?"

"We never left it. You played my old man like a champ."

"This is my house," she said sharply, "not the Triad office. I've no intention of listening while you insult me."

"Listen while I make you an offer, then."

"What kind of offer?"

"My brothers and I intend to sell Landon Enterprises."

"Is that supposed to mean something to me?"

"Only that we can't do it until Triad gets out of that sea of red ink it's floating in."

Eve smiled coolly. "My heart bleeds for you."

"Here's the deal," Zach said brusquely. "I'll let you run Triad but you'll have to answer to me on a daily basis."

Her heart leaped, but she folded her arms over her breasts and eyed him cautiously.

"Why? Why would you ask me to come back to work?"

"I just told you. Because I have to put Triad into the black. That next movie you're planning... What's it called?"

"*Hollywood Wedding*. But how did you...?"

"Did you think I've spent the week sitting in your office doing nothing? I know all your plans for Triad, Eve, even that you've already promised to spend money you don't yet have."

"Only because I'm convinced *Hollywood Wedding* will save the company."

Zach nodded. "How much do you need?"

She named a number that made his eyes widen, but he didn't flinch.

"I can raise it."

"You? But how could an accountant——?"

He laughed. "Is that what you think I am? Hell, baby, I'm a stockbroker. My specialty is researching investments for rich people and then convincing them to make them."

She couldn't help smiling. "I see."

"And before that, I was an arbitrageur. Do you know what that is?"

Eve shook her head and swiped the tip of her tongue over her dry lips. Everything was happening too fast. She felt the way she had the first time she'd gone skiing, out of control yet almost giddy with excitement.

"It's a guy who plays high-risk games with other people's money. If he's right, everybody makes a fortune. If he's wrong..."

This time, she laughed out loud. "It sounds a lot like making movies."

"Well?" His eyes met hers. "Is it a deal?"

Her heart was racing like a trapped bird's; she wanted to say yes, but how could she? She would be working with a man who despised her, who thought she'd been his father's playmate.

"I'll give you a contract that lasts until we finish making *Hollywood Wedding*. Now, answer me, Eve. Is it a go?"

The tip of her tongue swept across her lips again. She saw his eyes follow the simple gesture and she took a breath.

"I'd like to say yes, but——"

"But? What do you want, Eve? A percentage of profits? Well, why not? You'll work all the harder for a piece of the action."

"I just—I just don't see how we can work together as long as you think that I'm a woman who..."

She cried out as Zach swept her into his arms. His mouth dropped to hers in a kiss that was nothing but fierce masculine domination, and she struggled against it even as she felt the swift, answering rush of heat in her blood.

She whispered his name against his lips and instantly his kiss changed to something filled with a sweet passion that was her undoing.

Her arms rose and wound around his neck. He fell back against the wall, still holding her, his mouth hot over hers, his teeth and tongue branding her with his desire. His hand rose, cupped the fullness of her breast, and she moaned into his mouth.

The world dipped under her feet. When it settled again, Zach was holding her by the shoulders and looking into her eyes.

"It isn't an act," he said, his voice rough. "I thought it was, but hell, it isn't. You want me, Eve, and there's no point pretending I don't want you." He caught her wrist when she tried to turn away. "And that's my ace, baby. You won't be able to play your games with me. I've got your number, and I won't let you forget it."

Horror and despair made her throat tighten. "What kind of man are you?"

Zach laughed low in his throat. "The kind you wish had never driven into the middle of that movie set," he said as he let go of her. "Now, get yourself dressed. We're going out."

"No! That's not part of our deal."

"This is business, Eve. They're giving a going-away party for your pal Brubeck. I figure you can introduce me." He shot back his cuff and looked at his watch. "I'll pick you up in an hour."

"No. I'll—I'll meet you there."

He laughed. "And let you cut off some other poor bastard on the freeway? No, thanks, not so long as Triad's paying your insurance."

She knew immediately. "You?" she whispered, remembering the man in the Porsche.

"Me." His smile tilted. "It must be fate, Evie, keeps bringing us together." He reached out and brought her to him for one swift, hard kiss. Before she had time to react, he turned and strolled from the kitchen. Eve flew after him.

"Zach!"

He turned, his hand on the doorknob.

"Zach," she repeated. Her face was pale but she stood straight and tall. "I won't sleep with you."

He looked at her for a long minute, and then he smiled, opened the door and stepped outside.

"It's polite to wait until you're asked," he said, and the door swung shut.

Eve stared at it while the silence settled around her. Then she rushed forward, wrenched open the door and slammed it hard enough to rattle the frame.

With a toss of her head, she turned and marched into her bedroom.

CHAPTER FIVE

THE house stood on a hilltop, looking out over the Pacific. It was low and angular, a brilliantly lighted beacon against the dark night sky.

Zach chuckled as he turned into the driveway. "It looks like a spaceship, ready for takeoff."

"A cedar and glass spaceship," Eve said, smiling. Behind the house, hundreds of tiny white lights glowed in the trees, shimmering and shifting on the wind's breath. "But it's handsome, isn't it?"

Zach drove past the cars parked along the driveway.

"And cozy," he said with a wry smile as he pulled in between a Lamborghini and a Rolls. "Just the right setting for a casual poolside barbecue."

Eve laughed as she undid her seat belt. "I probably should have warned you that out here, casual only means you can leave off the tux."

"Yeah." Zach stepped from the Porsche, came around to her side of the car and opened the door. "Well, I took old Bob at his word. They're going to have to take me as I am."

She looked at him as she stepped from the car. He was wearing softly faded, snug-fitting Levi's, leather moccasins and a cream-colored shirt. His collar was open, exposing his throat; his sleeves were rolled back to show hard, muscular forearms. The light from the lampposts set along the driveway touched his brown hair with gold and amber, and there was a faint, tantalizing

79

scent about him, a combination of soap and lemon and clean, sexy male.

Eve felt a sudden tightness just behind her breastbone. She had been at a dozen parties like this one; she knew that the crowd would be studded with stars and wannabees. And yet Zach would be the man every female eye would seek out, the man other men would envy. He would turn heads by entering a room, not just because of his ruggedly masculine good looks but because of what emanated from him, that aura of arrogance and power she found so infuriating.

It was an aura other women might be foolish enough to find intriguing, but not she. She would never—she could never...

"Well?"

Eve blinked. Her gaze shot to Zach's. He was watching her through eyes that were dark and unreadable. A little smile crooked at the corner of his mouth, and suddenly she thought of how it had felt when his mouth crushed down on hers, when his body had pressed, hot and hard, against hers....

"Now that you've taken the time to look me over, will I do?"

She fought for breath as the fist squeezed her heart again. It took all her strength to smile brightly and lift her shoulders in an unconcerned shrug.

"Of course," she said briskly. "Besides, by midnight the place will be so crowded people will be standing on top of each other. Nobody'll be able to see what anybody's wearing."

A car horn beeped behind them. Zach glanced over his shoulder, put his arm lightly around Eve's waist and drew her out of the path of a Mercedes.

"In that case," he said, smiling at her, "I'm glad I got a look at you before midnight. You look lovely tonight, Eve."

The compliment had been automatic, the kind of thing a man said to a woman on an evening out, but Zach regretted it as soon as he'd offered it. *This* wasn't an evening out, it was a business arrangement, plain and simple. And Eve was a woman who probably collected praise from men the way some people collected stamps.

And yet, he thought as he looked at her, what he'd told her was true. She did look lovely. More than lovely. She was wearing a blue dress that turned her eyes the color of violets and her hair a shade of gold that was so pure it dazzled his eyes. His gaze fell to her mouth, pale and pink and soft, and he thought of how it would feel beneath his, of how it would be to take her in his arms right now.

"I mean," he said, hurrying the words, gathering them around him to cloak the direction his thoughts had been taking, "I had no idea what people wear for a night out in Tinseltown."

Eve smiled as they reached the steps that led to the front door.

"Everything," she said, "and anything. From the sublime to the ridiculous, and back again. Sometimes, the password seems to be, the more outrageous, the bet——"

Above them, the door flew open. A couple came racing out of the house, laughing, and tripped down the steps arm in arm.

The woman, blazing with diamonds, looked as if she'd been poured into her skintight leather bustier, matching short shorts and black fishnet stockings. There were laced granny boots on her feet, the heels as high and slim as stilettos.

The man was every bit as exotic-looking as his companion. Gold and silver hoops bristled in his ears. Chartreuse silk jeans were tucked into his lizard-skin combat boots, and his fuchsia jacket was only a shade or two brighter than his spiked hair.

"You're late," the woman said gaily, "at least half a dozen glasses of Dom Perignon behind the rest of the crowd."

Zach laughed and drew Eve out of their path. "We'll do our best to catch up."

Eve grinned wickedly as the duo sped past them.

"See what I mean?" she whispered. "In this town, anything goes!"

Laughing, they stepped through the door.

Zach's first thought was that they'd blundered into a mirrored anthill.

"My God," he said, "there must be a couple of hundred people packed inside this room."

Eve frowned, shook her head and leaned closer.

"I can't hear you."

Of course, she couldn't. The music was blasting away, the beat so loud that Zach could feel it vibrating through the floor. He drew her closer to his side.

"I said," he shouted, "I've never seen so many people in one place in my life, except maybe on a subway train at rush hour."

Eve laughed and said something, but it was Zach who shook his head this time. She rose on tiptoe and put her lips close to his ear. Her breath was warm, and he felt a ripple of electricity dance along his skin as she spoke.

"It'll be better once we get out on the terrace," she told him. "It's never as crowded outside as it is inside."

He drew back and gave her a puzzled smile. "I thought this was supposed to be a barbecue."

"Sure. But it's still early." Eve grinned. "It takes a while before people are desperate enough to trade the air-conditioning for the mosquitoes."

A white-coated waiter edged through the crowd toward them, paused and said something. Zach couldn't hear a word but the tray the waiter held out, filled with flutes of champagne and rounds of caviar-heaped toast, spoke volumes.

"Eve?"

She nodded, and he took two glasses of champagne and handed her one. He reached for the caviar, too, but she put her hand lightly on his arm and shook her head.

"I never eat the stuff."

She was smiling at him, her eyes as blue as a tropical sea, and Zach felt his throat constrict.

"I couldn't hear you," he said, lying straight through his teeth, but it was worth it. Eve leaned towards him, stood on her toes again and brought her lips to his ear.

She said something about knowing it was silly but not being able to get past the thought that caviar was just a fancy name for fish eggs. Zach laughed, because he was supposed to, but all he could concentrate on was the feel of her breath against his skin and the scent of her rising to his nostrils, a sweet fragrance that was composed of equal parts spring flowers and luscious woman.

She drew back, laughing, and after a second he laughed, too, because he figured that was what he was supposed to do, and he wondered how in hell he was going to go on standing here like this, packed in so tightly against this woman that he could feel the press of her breasts against him, without losing his mind.

"...do you think so far?"

He cleared his throat. The music had dipped to a level with only slightly fewer decibels than the SST on takeoff and conversation had suddenly become possible.

"Sorry," he said, "I missed that."

"I said, what do you think of a simple poolside barbecue, Hollywood style?"

Zach smiled. "Well, I haven't seen the pool."

"Trust me. There's a pool. And it's Olympic-size."

"You've been here before?"

"No. But I've been out here long enough to know how the rich and famous live. Their houses are spectacular, their pools can float the QEII, and the parties they throw would make Nero jealous."

What would make Nero jealous, Zach thought, was Eve. In this room filled with beautiful women who made their fortunes by being beautiful, she was the only one any man worth the name would notice.

And they had noticed. He could see the glances that kept coming her way, the interested assessments being made by all those masculine eyes...

"Eve!"

A man was pushing through the crowd toward them. He was tall, with the rangy good looks of an Eastwood or a Connery.

"Dex," Eve said in surprise, and then the man gathered her in his arms and kissed her.

Zach felt his entire body tense with fury. He watched as Eve's head fell back, as her hands flattened against the man's chest. Was that how she'd looked when she'd kissed him? Zach's eyes narrowed as he looked at the man. *You son of a bitch,* he thought, *I'll kill you if you don't let go of her.*

"Dex," Eve said again. She had stepped back, still in the circle of the man's arms. Her face was flushed.

Look at her, Zach thought, hell, look at her.

"You look gorgeous as always, Eve. But where have you been keeping yourself?"

"Dex." She looked at Zach. "I'd like you to meet Zachary Landon. Zach is——"

"Eve's employer," Zach said. "Her boss. The one who makes the decisions at Triad now."

Eve's face went blank. "Yes," she said, "that's right. Zach's come out here to run things."

"Is that so?" Dex smiled politely. "Well, welcome to Hollywood, old man." He chucked Eve under the chin. "You're fortunate, having Eve to show you around."

"Yes." Zach's lips drew back from his teeth. "Yes, I'm sure I am."

"Yeah," Dex said absently. He looked over Zach's shoulder, smiled and waved his hand in the air. "There's Steven," he said. "I want to talk to him about his next film. Give me a call, Eve, will you?"

"Yes," she said politely. "I will." He bent to kiss her and she turned her head so that his mouth brushed her cheek. "Take care, Dex." As soon as he was gone, she looked at Zach. "What was that all about?"

He could feel the stiffness of the smile that curved across his lips.

"I'm impressed," he said. "You've got some high-visibility scalps hanging from your belt."

Eve's face whitened. "Maybe you'd like to clarify that remark."

Zach shrugged. He could feel his hand tightening around his champagne glass.

"I'm just impressed by the variety of friends you have, Eve, that's all."

"Just remember something, Zach. It wasn't my idea to come here tonight, it was yours, just as it was your idea to ask me to come back to work at Triad."

He took a deep breath. What was the matter with him? She was right. And anyway, her relationships with men were her own business. She could sleep with every actor in Hollywood, for all he gave a damn.

"Okay. I was out of line."

"I may work for you, Zach," she said, her voice taut, "but I don't have to take your insults."

"Look, I apologized. Now, let's forget about it, Okay?"

The music suddenly swelled, the beat of drums and guitars drowning out everything, and Eve took refuge in the noise.

She knew what she ought to tell Zach to do with his lukewarm apology.

It was insane, to do anything less.

She knew him for what he was, an egotistical, too-handsome, too-rich-for-his-own-good rat. He'd made up his mind about her before he'd even met her. As far as he was concerned, she was a tramp who'd traded her favors for a career and could never be trusted not to go on trading them for whatever else she might want.

Eve took a shuddering breath. That his touch could excite her, that his kisses could turn her to flame, only made the situation worse. It was like discovering some awful weakness within herself, one that was as fascinating as it was frightening.

But it would be even worse to walk away from Triad now, with the prize so near at hand. She had spent her life trying to prove herself, and now here it was, the chance to show all the Zach Landons of this world who she really was and what she could accomplish....

A roar of laughter rose over the music. Startled, Eve looked up.

"What's happening?" she said.

Zach put his arm around her waist as the surge of the crowd pressed them closer together.

"I don't know. I can't——" He stood on his toes and began to laugh. "I don't believe it."

"Don't believe what?"

"There's a chimpanzee wearing tails and a top hat in the next room. It looks as if he's handing out party favors."

"Believe it," Eve said with a weary smile. "The first party I went to out here, a seal jumped into the pool and played water polo with the guests."

Zach drew her more closely into the circle of his arm. "Will you look at that? Somebody left us an empty corner." He grinned as he tucked Eve safely against him. "There must be all of two square inches here, and it's all ours."

Two inches wasn't much of an exaggeration, she thought. She was standing so close to Zach she could hardly tell where his body began and hers ended.

No. Her breath caught. That wasn't true. It was easy to tell. He was hard where she was soft, big where she was small. His hand lay lightly on her waist but she could feel the power of it, and the heat....

"Seals and chimps, huh?" She looked up. Zach was smiling at her. It would take only the simplest movement to lift her hand to his cheek.... "What else goes on at these shindigs?"

Eve told him. She dredged up every strange, funny story she'd ever heard. If she could keep talking, keep him laughing, then maybe she could stop thinking about how it would feel if he suddenly gathered her into his arms and kissed her....

Keep smiling, Zach told himself, keep laughing, Landon, even if it feels as if the muscles in your face are freezing, even if you don't know what in hell the woman leaning against you is saying.

He could hardly feel the weight of her, but that didn't keep him from being aware of every soft, feminine inch. Her breasts brushed his chest, her belly brushed his loins, and if he didn't find a way to move away from her soon, he was going to disgrace himself.

What the hell was this? He was not a randy kid. Eve was attractive, yes. A man would have to be dead not to see that, but so what? This room was full of attractive women. The world was full of them.

He'd married one, hadn't he?

Eve was telling him another story, something about a basketball tournament between starlets. Her face was animated, her cheeks flushed with color. She laughed softly and tilted her head back, exposing the long, clean line of her throat, and he had to fight the urge to bend his head, to touch his mouth to that throat....

A man balancing a pair of highball glasses filled to the brim with amber liquid edged past them. Eve moved closer, although Zach wouldn't have thought it was possible. She lay her hand on his arm for balance.

He looked down at her fingers with their ivory-tipped nails and wondered what she would do if he took her hand, brought it to his body and let her feel exactly what she was doing to him.

Zach stifled a groan. *Hell,* he thought, *oh, hell. You're being an ass, Landon. Think about something else. Think about—about what Eve's telling you. Concentrate, dammit. Concentrate!*

He forced himself to hear her voice, not just as a soft, musical drone but to hear the words.

"And then," she said, "I thought, who's kidding who? This isn't just ridiculous, it's audacious."

"Audacious," Zach repeated stupidly, nodding his head as if he had a clue to what she was saying.

She smiled, and he watched the way her lips curved in a soft, sweet line. Her mouth was a deep, lush pink, her teeth white and perfect. He remembered the taste of those lips, wondered how it would feel if those teeth closed lightly on his flesh in the heat of passion.

Dammit, was he crazy? He knew what this woman was. He'd been married to one like her—although compared to Eve, his former wife was an amateur. Eve was twice as beautiful and ten times more devious. Just look at the games she'd played with his father....

"...pointless to pretend it wasn't happening," she said, and laughed. "We both knew it. What was the point in playing games? So I took a deep breath and I said..."

"You said, this is all a waste of time." Zach's voice, harsh and edged, rasped from his throat. "You said, why don't we cut to the chase, Tom? Or Dick, or Harry, or maybe it was even Ed. You said, I want something from you, you want something from me, so let's just go back to my place or yours, take off our clothes, get into bed and——"

He stopped, stunned by his own cruelty, by his coarseness—and by the shock and horror registering on Eve's face.

"Eve," he said, reaching out his hand, "Eve——"

But she was already gone, spinning away from him and pushing through the crowd that still thronged the room.

Zach cursed himself for a fool and went after her.

"Eve!"

She couldn't hear him, or didn't want to. He couldn't tell which. The music was blasting loudly again and the noise of the crowd was almost unbearable.

"Eve, wait!"

She was still ahead of him, a blur of golden hair and a flash of blue skirt. He shoved past a knot of people blocking the open doors to the brick patio and broke free into the night.

Where in hell was she?

Zach stood still and looked around him. Eve had been right; it wasn't half as crowded out here. People were standing around in little clusters, talking and drinking, and he could see that she was not one of them.

There was an enormous pool off to his right, rimmed on one side by a series of pseudo thatched-roof huts he supposed were dressing rooms. A bar and a series of elaborate buffet table were behind the pool, and a DJ in a flowered Hawaiian shirt and candy-striped shorts was working his ear-splitting magic over a pyramid of audio equipment beside a parquet dance floor just to the left.

And, beyond that, where steps led down from the deck and fell away into darkness, he saw a flutter of blue and gold.

"Eve," Zach said harshly, and set off after her.

He caught her at the bottom of the steps, clasping her shoulders and whirling her toward him.

"Let go of me!"

"Listen to me, Eve."

"No!" She pounded her fists against his shoulders. "You bastard, let me go!"

"Eve!" Zach trapped her hands in his and dragged them down the sides of her body. "Dammit, will you listen?"

"I did listen! But I'm not going to anymore."

She was panting now, and struggling, and he fell back against the wide trunk of a eucalyptus tree and took her with him, wedging her between his legs in an effort to keep her still.

"I should never have said what I did. It was wrong, I know it was." Zach clasped her face in his hands. "Dammit," he said gruffly, "will you look at me? I'm trying to apologize."

"You already did that once tonight, remember? And I, like a fool, let you." Eve wrapped her hands around his wrists and tried to break free of his iron-hard grasp, but it was useless. "Let go of me, Zach!"

"Eve, hell, I don't know why I said——"

"It's because you're an insulting, domineering, insensitive son of a bitch!"

"Yes. All right. I'm not denying——"

"And stupid," she said, trying not to let loose the tears building inside her even though they were surely just tears of anger. "Blind, dumb, male stupid!"

"Yes. I admit it. It's just that—that I was standing there going crazy, thinking about how every man inside that damned room wanted you——"

"You *are* crazy! Did you see who's at this party tonight? Did you take a good, hard look?"

Zach's thumbs traced the high, delicate arcs of her cheekbones.

"—and of how glad you were to see that macho bag of wind, Dex Burton——"

"Dex Burton?" Eve almost laughed. "He makes me sick to my stomach."

Zach's mouth twisted. "That was some greeting to give a guy who makes you sick to your stomach."

"Dex practically mugged me! He grabbed me before I could do anything to stop him—and how *could* I have stopped him, when we were packed in like sardines in a tin?"

"But I saw——"

"You're a fool, Zachary Landon, that's what you are." Her voice cracked. "A damned miserable fool."

He drew back a little, his hands still cupping her face.

"Yes." His voice was very low. "Yes, I think I am."

Eve took a deep breath. "I want to go home now."

"No."

"Fine. You stay and have a good time. I'll take a taxi."

Zach turned with Eve still in his arms, so that now it was she who was leaning against the tree.

"No," he whispered, and his hands slid down and cupped her shoulders.

"What do you mean, no? The night's over, and so is our deal. I'd sooner work for the devil himself than——"

The rest of her words were lost as his mouth took hers.

Eve was not a child. She was a woman and she had been kissed before. By boys, by men—even, on more than one occasion, by screen legends whose kisses should have been enough to have set her world spinning.

It had never happened—until now.

His kiss was harsh and demanding, forged in fire and tasting of hunger and passion, and she tried to resist it, standing rigid in his embrace while her brain shrieked a warning. But it was her body that was reacting, with a primitive need as old as time.

In less time than it took for her heart to send the blood surging through her veins, she was on fire.

She whimpered, rose on tiptoe and curled her arms around his neck, drawing his face closer to hers, her lips parting to the searing thrust of his tongue.

Yes, she thought, yes, oh, yes. This was what she wanted, this was who she'd wanted. The man in her arms was everything, and she would not deny him or herself.

Zach groaned against her mouth. His arms tightened around her and he swept her closer, one hand pressed into the small of her back to tilt her hips to his, the other fisted in her hair while he kissed her again and again.

He said something, or she thought he did. She couldn't tell, couldn't think. Not anymore. She was nothing but shimmering sensation.

Zach bent his head, closed his teeth lightly on the tender skin of her throat. She moaned, threaded her fingers into his hair, guided him as he kissed his way over the curve of her breast to her nipple.

The soft cotton of her skirt bunched in his hands. He slid the skirt up her legs and she whimpered as his fingers, cool as the night air, brushed across her thighs.

"Eve," he said, "oh, God, Eve..."

Her breath caught in her throat. His hands skimmed over her silk panties, his touch feather light, but she felt the immediate, answering throb of desire begin beating deep inside her. He whispered her name again, cupped her bottom and lifted her into the hardness and heat of his erection, and then his fingers slid under the silk and touched her flesh.

She cried out in passion. Her head fell back and her hands dug hard into his shoulders, and he bent to her, seeking her mouth and, when he found it, ravishing it with his.

Eve's response was almost Zach's undoing. She was sobbing in his arms, kissing him with an openmouthed frenzy. And she was hot, so hot; her skin burned against his. He moved against her, blindly seeking her warmth, aching now to bury himself within the velvet dampness he knew awaited him.

He caught her hand, brought it down to him, pressed her palm over his jeans, over his straining erection. Her fingers curled over him and he groaned and pressed feverishly against her hand, wanting her to touch him yet knowing what would happen if he let her go on touching him.

He was losing control. Hell, he was out of control, in a way he had never been, not even when he was a boy. And he didn't want that, didn't want this to end here, with him straining against her hand instead of buried deep within her heat and softness.

"Zach," she whispered, "oh, please, Zach, please..."

Suddenly, the sky lit above them. Blue and red flame streamed out across the darkness.

Eve cried out, and Zach drew her close.

"It's nothing," he whispered. "It's only fireworks, Eve."

The sky lit again, and this time she could feel the deep, primal roar of the explosion vibrate through her bones.

"Don't be afraid," Zach whispered, his mouth at her throat.

Fireworks, she thought. Fireworks, explosive, hot and brilliant...

And then gone, leaving nothing behind but wisps of trailing smoke.

She went rigid in Zach's arms.

"Eve?"

"Stop it," she said.

"Eve, baby..."

She struck out at him blindly, her blows fierce against his shoulders and chest.

"Get away from me, damn you!"

The night sky, alive with shining bursts of flame, seemed to have drained the color from her face. The passion that had lit her eyes was gone. All Zach could see in them now was disgust, and suddenly all his hunger was gone, replaced by more than enough self-loathing for the both of them.

His hands fell to his sides and he took a step back.

"I'll take you home," he said tonelessly.

Eve didn't answer. She straightened her dress, ran her fingers through her hair and walked off into the darkness.

Zach took a deep breath. He waited a moment and then followed after her.

CHAPTER SIX

ZACH came through the door of his suite, tossed his keys on the coffee table and reached for the phone. By the time room service answered, he'd already pulled off his jacket and his tie.

"Yeah," he said, as he unbuttoned his shirt, "this is Suite 708. How long to send up a bottle of Rolling Rock, a hamburger, an order of French fries and a tossed salad?" He nodded. "Half an hour's fine. On second thought, better make that two beers."

By the time the waiter wheeled in his dinner—if you could call a hamburger dinner, Zach thought with a grimace—he'd showered and changed to a pair of cutoff denims, sneakers and a navy blue T-shirt. He signed the check, saw the waiter out, turned the TV to something mindless and sank down on the sitting-room sofa to eat his first bite of food in hours.

The hamburger was charred on the outside, raw in the middle and generally tasted as if it had been cooked sometime last Tuesday. Zach dumped it back on his plate and reached instead for a bottle of Rolling Rock.

The beer, cold and crisp, was just what he needed after his endless day in the salt mines. He sighed, lay his head back against the sofa and put his feet up on the coffee table.

Amazing, how much a producer's job involved. Zach tilted the bottle to his lips again. Somewhere he'd gotten the idea a producer just signed checks. The fact was that every problem ended up on his desk, now that Eve...

Zach frowned. Never mind. What mattered was that *The Ghost Stallion* was finally wrapped, or in the can, or whatever it was you said when a movie was done. He still had trouble with the lingo, but considering that the time he'd been out here gave new meaning to the concept of on-the-job training, not speaking the jargon was the least of his problems.

"The very least," he muttered, putting down the bottle and reaching for the French fries. He bit into one, made a face and reached for the beer again.

At least Eve was out of the picture. That was something to be grateful for. How he'd ever convinced himself she could possibly help him sort his way through the orchestrated chaos of making a film still amazed him.

Zach aimed the remote control at the TV and clicked it to silence. Then he rose, went into the bedroom and took his laptop computer from the closet. He sat down on the edge of the king-size bed, turned on the computer, plugged its modem into the telephone jack and punched up the screen.

Whatever talent Eve Palmer had for running a business was second-best to the talent she had for screwing up a man's head. Her blend of beauty and brains and hot-blooded sexuality was...

The computer screen filled with numbers and graphs. Zach frowned, scanned them, then scrolled to the next screen. After a couple of minutes, he relaxed.

At least all was well on the home front. Not that he'd expected anything less. He didn't need to be in the office to stay on top of things, not in this age of computers and faxes and modems. Besides, Jason Emery, his second-in-command back in Boston, was more than capable of holding down the fort.

He typed a quick E-mail note for Jace, added some instructions to be carried out at tomorrow's market opening, then signed off and unplugged the modem. It was good to know that Landon Brokerage was riding the waves.

His smile faded as he made his way back to the sitting room and sank down on the sofa again. If only he could say the same for Triad.

He reached for the salad, but it looked as wilted as he felt. With a sigh, he pushed it aside, picked up the second bottle of beer and took a long, cool drink.

He'd spent every day of the past week either in that hovel of an office or on location, and Triad's problems were as miserable as ever. He couldn't even take credit for finishing *The Ghost Stallion*. Except for lowering the hammer on the little twerp with the goatee when his ego got in the way of reality, Zach knew he'd been little more than a bystander.

He took another drink, then lay his head back. Goodbye, Francis Cranshaw and Horace the Wonder Horse. Hello, *Hollywood Wedding*.

Damn, what a mess.

His mess, he thought, heaving a sigh. Eve had committed virtually all the company's credit to the film, a stupid move if ever he'd seen one. And he was stuck with the result, a bunch of signed contracts tying him to a script, a director, a set designer, camera operators, light men, sound men and who in hell knew what else. He had a leading lady—not a bad start for what was basically a two-character script, Zach thought wryly.

But he didn't have a director, or a location, and he didn't have a leading man—details that had apparently escaped Eve's attention.

"What the hell is this?" he'd roared at Emma when he'd realized the problem. "Didn't your boss notice something was missing?"

"I wouldn't know anything about that, sir," Emma had said coldly. "You'd have to ask her yourself."

Zach sat up and drank down the rest of the beer. He'd sooner have asked Horace the Wonder Horse a question before asking one of Eve. The only good thing that had happened lately was that she'd had the good sense to clear out.

He had not seen her since the night of the party, nor had he expected to. A woman who first reduced a man to a panting teenager and then damned near tossed a bucket of iced water over his head would have the brains to know that her career as his assistant was over.

The next morning, he'd written her a check for three months' pay, added a note reaffirming his verbal promise to pay her a percentage of profits from *Hollywood Wedding*—which was the equivalent of promising to pay bonuses to Eskimos who bought freezer chests—and sent the package off by special messenger.

It had come back with the same messenger. Zach had not been impressed by the gesture. All he cared about was that he'd closed the books on Eve Palmer.

He certainly didn't need her to help him run Triad. Learning the movie business was no mystery. You asked questions, you observed, you learned. And if things took a little longer that way—if they took a little longer...

"Dammit!"

Zach slammed the empty bottle on the coffee table. Who was he kidding? This business was as tricky as any he'd ever seen. How was he supposed to know who to hire as a male lead for *Hollywood Wedding?* The script called for a man in his late thirties, but what did that mean? A younger Paul Newman? An older Tom Cruise? Zach had no idea, and the director was no help. Zach had asked his advice, and the guy had almost frothed at the mouth.

"Get me Mel Gibson," he'd gushed.

Even Zach knew enough to laugh. If Triad went in hock for the next fifty years, Gibson would still be an unattainable dream.

And his boast to Eve, about getting big spenders to invest their money, had turned out to be hollow. All the big spenders he'd approached wanted to know who was starring in the film before they sank any money into it. And most of them wanted to know what had happened to Eve.

One or two of them had asked the question with a wink—which had, for some reason, made him want to punch out their lights. But a surprising number of others had said Eve had turned out to be more knowledgeable than they'd expected and that they were sure her expertise would be missed.

Ed Brubeck—who'd turned out to be fifty, jovial and gay, Zach thought with a grim smile—had been more direct.

"Nobody's going to put money into a ship without a rudder, Mr. Landon," he'd said.

Had Eve really been that rudder?

No. No, she couldn't. The old man had given her her job at Triad as a gift....

Or had he? Would Charles really have done that? His father had been a lot of things, but never stupid and certainly never sentimental.

Zach put his head in his hands. He'd never even considered that possibility, but then, it had all seemed so obvious just a short time ago. Now—now, he wasn't sure of anything, certainly not of the route Eve Palmer had taken to the top....

Or of why he couldn't get her out of his head.

"Dammit!"

He grabbed the remote control and aimed it at the TV. A sitcom came on, something that looked as stupid as he felt. He hit the mute button, swung his legs up on the sofa and stretched out, his arms beneath his head.

He had faced trouble before, and gotten out of it. There had to be a way.

By midnight, he still hadn't found it. The hands of the clock hit one, then two. Zach's eyelids drooped. Seconds later, he was asleep.

Zach shot upright. He was in total darkness except for a hissing black and white square hovering a couple of feet off the ground, and there was an incessant ringing noise someplace just behind his head.

The phone.

He grunted, swung his feet off the sofa and felt around on the table beside him. Something crashed to the floor but he ignored it and dragged the phone to his ear.

"Zach?"

The remote was under his butt. He dredged it out, aimed it at the TV screen and watched the picture disappear.

"Yes," he grunted. "Who the hell is this?"

"Is that any way to say hello to your big brother?"

"Grant?"

"On the nose, buddy. How you doing?"

Zach groped for the lamp, hit the switch and blinked when the room filled with light. He looked at his watch and groaned.

"Grant, do you know what time it is?"

"Sure. A little past seven."

"In New York, maybe. Now try deducting three hours and see what you come up with."

"Oh, man," Grant said. "I'm sorry. I forgot the time difference." A smile crept into his voice. "I'll bet you just got to bed, too."

Zach sighed. "You got that right."

"Party time, huh?" Grant said, chuckling.

Zach shut his eyes, leaned back and massaged his temples.

"Listen, pal, it's great to hear your voice, but why are you calling?" His eyes flew open. "If this is some gag you and Cade cooked up..."

"No. This is for real." The humor had left Grant's voice. "Zach? You recall the time we talked about how to score in the market?"

Zach sighed. "You're telling me you need stock market advice at four in the bloody a.m.?"

"You said something about knowing when it was time to cut your losses."

"Yeah. I told you that only the true believers and the certifiably insane don't know when it's time to cut their losses and get out." He chuckled. "Hey, man, I charge my clients a lot of dough for those words of wisdom."

"It's good advice, right? I mean, you wouldn't think a man was admitting defeat if——"

"Grant?" Zach was wide awake now. "Are you in financial trouble?"

"No, nothing like that. It's—it's this guardianship..." Grant's inhalation sounded harsh. "My ward isn't—she isn't twelve."

"She's younger?"

"Older. She's not a girl, Zach. She's a woman, and——"

Zach got to his feet. "And," he said, his voice harsh, "she's doing a number on your head."

Grant made a sound Zach figured was supposed to be a laugh.

"Yeah."

"*Cherchez la femme,* old buddy," Zach said, closing his eyes. "Look out for the female of the species. Whenever there's trouble, there's a dame in the picture." He sighed, pinched the bridge of his nose and sank down on the sofa again. "Do yourself a favor, man. Hand the babe off to some other sap."

"I thought of that, but I signed on for this and——"

"Well, sign off! Cut your losses, remember?"

"Zach? Are you okay? You sound funny."

"Sure," Zach said quickly. "This production company is all screwed up, that's all, and—and listen, brother mine, I've got a breakfast meeting this a.m. and if I want to be my usual brilliant self..."

"Sure. Get some shut-eye. And thanks for the advice."

"Yeah. Just be sure you take it. When in doubt, cut your losses."

Grant chuckled. "And run."

Zach hung up the phone, walked to the window and looked out over the sleeping city. He knew the answer to his problems. It was as clear as if somebody had scrawled it across the smoggy sky.

It was just that he wasn't very good at eating crow, but crow wouldn't taste much worse than turkey and a turkey was what he was going to have on his hands if *Hollywood Wedding* was a failure.

He turned from the window and glanced at his watch. It was pushing five o'clock. Time for a shave, a shower, a pot of black coffee and then...

Then, he thought with a sigh, he'd have that breakfast meeting. It wasn't one he'd planned on, but so what?

A little risk put spice in a man's life.

Eve was in the shower when she heard the distant tinkling of the phone.

Let the answering machine take the call, she thought, tilting her head to the spray. Anybody who telephoned this early in the morning deserved to speak to a machine.

Besides, phone calls at this hour meant someone was having a crisis. And she wasn't in the mood for anybody's crisis but her own.

It was amazing, how one person could come busting into your life and turn it upside down, but that was what Zachary Landon had done. In no time at all, he'd humiliated her personally and ruined her professionally—and the worst of it was, she'd helped him do it.

Eve shut off the shower, slid open the stall door and stepped onto the bath mat. How could she have been such a fool that night? She'd thought about it endlessly as she'd gone from fruitless job interview to interview, and she was no closer to an answer now than she'd been days ago.

Zach had come on to her, but so what? Men had been coming on to her for years, starting with dear old foster Dad, but she was an adult now; she knew how to deal with the problem.

A chilly look, an even chillier remark, she thought as she pulled on a pair of baggy sweatpants and an even baggier sweatshirt, and, if necessary, a swift kick where it would do the most good, were enough to stop the most relentless would-be Don Juan.

So what had gone wrong? She had given Zach enough cool looks to freeze water, said enough nasty things to have sent him running...

Yes, but she certainly hadn't kicked him. Eve stared at herself in the mirror as she brushed her hair from her face. No, she hadn't kicked him at all. Instead, she'd gone crazy in his arms, reacted to his kisses and to his touch in a way she had never even dreamed of reacting.

And Zach had counted on that, she reminded herself grimly as she pulled her hair into a ponytail. He'd made his position painfully clear with all that rot about having her number and knowing she wanted him... Which, of course, was untrue.

The man was a consummate seducer, smooth and experienced with women. He'd set out to humiliate her, and he'd succeeded. Admirably.

Eve shut off the bathroom light and strode briskly down the hall to the kitchen. As for what had happened the next day—well, she had no one but herself to blame for that. Quitting her job had been one thing, but sending back the check Zach had sent had been just plain stupid. Triad owed her that money, dammit. She'd worked hard, and now what did she have to show for her efforts?

She yanked open the refrigerator door, peered inside at the almost empty shelves and sighed. Nothing, that was what. She had little money, no job, no prospects...

The telephone rang again. Eve glanced at the clock. It was still early, but you never could tell. Someone might be calling about a job. She'd sat through half a dozen interviews; maybe one was going to pay off, she thought, and picked up the handset.

"Hello?"

"Hello, Eve."

It was the last voice in the world she wanted to hear, the last voice she'd ever thought to hear again. For an instant, she was too shocked to react.

"It's Zach."

"I know who it is. What do you want?"

"I left a message on your machine a little while ago. Didn't you get it?"

"No. And I'm not interested in getting it. I've nothing to say to you."

"Look, I know we didn't part amicably——"

Eve laughed.

"All right, dammit, so we parted badly."

"Badly?" Eve shook her head. "You have a talent for understatement."

"Eve, we have to talk."

"We are talking, much to my regret. In fact, I don't see any reason for this conversation, so good——"

"Wait! Don't hang up, dammit. I...I..." His breath rasped sharply through the phone. "Listen, have you had breakfast yet?"

"Have I what?" she said, and laughed.

"Do us both a favor, okay? I haven't had much sleep, my stomach's growling, and my disposition's shot to hell."

"What a pity."

"Just answer the question. Have you eaten yet?"

"No. And now I probably won't. Hearing your voice has just about ruined my appetite."

"For whatever it's worth, Eve, this isn't easy for me."

"You're breaking my heart."

"I'll pick you up in half an hour. Where shall I make a reservation? The Polo Lounge?"

Eve took a deep breath. "Let me say this in words of one syllable, so there's no danger of you not understanding. I do not like you. In fact, it would not be overstating things if I said I hated your guts. Is that clear?"

He gave a sharp laugh. "As glass."

"Good. I'm glad we agree on something."

"We can agree on more than that, if you give me the chance." There was a silence, and then Zach cleared his throat. "I was wrong. About you not being capable——"

"You're repeating yourself, Zach. I heard this speech before."

"No. You never heard me say that—that I was wrong about why my old man put you in charge of Triad."

Eve knew it was a moment for some clever, biting retort but she was speechless. Say something, she told herself fiercely. She swallowed hard, took a breath and spoke.

"If you're waiting to hear the sound of my knees hitting the floor in gratitude——"

"Look, I know you think this is too little, too late, but at least hear me out."

"Why should I?"

Because Triad needs you, Zach thought, but he knew there was more to it than that. He wanted Eve beside him. He didn't entirely trust her, she could infuriate him with a look or a word—but like the yin and the yang of the world, she could also make him feel more alive than he had in a long, long time.

"Because I need your help." There was silence on the phone, and he spoke quickly, afraid she was going to hang up. "Eve." His voice took on a softer tone. "Have breakfast with me. Please."

Eve hesitated. What could be more harmless than breakfast?

"All right," she said. "Pick a place and I'll meet you."

Zach let out his breath. "How about the Polo Lounge?"

The Polo Lounge? It was the place for power breakfasts, where Hollywood's elite drank their decaf, buttered their toast and agreed to multimillion-dollar deals.

No, Eve thought, not the lounge. If he'd set out to confuse her, he'd more than succeeded. She'd meet him someplace simple and down-to-earth, someplace where his brand of bull wouldn't mean a thing.

"There's a place just a couple of blocks north of my apartment," she said. "You can't miss it."

"What's it called?"

Eve smiled. "El Mirador," she said, and hung up.

He was waiting for her when she got there, leaning against his Porsche with his arms crossed over his chest, and she knew right away that if she'd thought to put him in his place by meeting him at a taco stand, she'd made a mistake.

Zach was a man who'd dominate any setting, and that was what he was doing now. Dressed casually, in chinos and a navy blazer over a white shirt worn open at the throat, he looked more handsome and masculine than any man had a right to look.

Her heart did a quick two-step that sent it knocking against her ribs.

He smiled as she walked toward him, his green eyes reflecting as much amusement as irritation. He straightened up and came toward her, his gaze flickering over her, and she almost regretted that she hadn't bothered changing out of her sweatsuit or that she hadn't at least brushed out her hair and put on some makeup.

But then she remembered exactly what kind of man Zach Landon was and that they'd played this game before, and her regrets faded away.

He jerked his chin toward the pink and purple flowered awning behind her.

"El Mirador, hmm?" he said.

Eve shrugged. "Rumor has it that Michelin's about to give the place a gold star."

To her surprise, he laughed. "Well, the food can't be any worse than the stuff my hotel serves." He took her arm, his grasp just tight enough to keep her from jerking away, and led her to the counter. "What do you recommend?"

"Arsenic," she said sweetly.

Zach ignored her and scanned the hand-printed menu wall. "We'll have the mangoes," he told the counterman, "and then the *ranchos huevos*. Oh, and two large coffees." He shot Eve a smile as he paid for their meal. "We can have champagne later, to celebrate."

"Don't talk like a fool, Zach. I can't imagine we'd ever have anything to celebrate."

Zach laughed, but he didn't answer. It was safer that way, because the thought occurred to him that she was probably right, he was a fool—a fool to involve himself with Eve again.

She had not taken any pains at all for this meeting, that was obvious. She was dressed in an outfit as sexily stylish as a paper bag, her face was shiny and untouched by makeup, her hair was yanked back in a ponytail, and she was treating him as if he was the bearer of bubonic plague.

In short, everything about her said she hated him. But none of it made her any less desirable.

The baggy pants only made a man wonder at the long length of the legs hidden inside. The oversize shirt lent an air of sweet mystery to the faint, high thrust of her breasts. As for makeup—why would she need it? Her eyes couldn't be more blue, and her mouth was already the soft pink of dawn.

She didn't need any artifice at all, not even perfume. Her own scent, clean and fragrant as a flower, rose to his nostrils and dazzled him. He wanted to pull her closer and bury his nose in her hair to inhale her essence, lift her face to his and taste her mouth...

"Señor?"

Zach looked up. The counterman was shoving a tray toward him. He hefted it in one hand, kept a grip on Eve's elbow with the other and led her to a wooden table sporting a Corona beer umbrella.

Eve yanked free and settled herself on the bench. Zach sat down opposite her.

"What is it you want, Zach?"

"First we eat, then we talk."

She watched in stony silence as he stabbed a plastic fork into the eggs and lifted it to his mouth. "Mmm," he said. "Hey, that's not bad." He took another bite, then took a sip of coffee. "Not bad at all."

Eve swallowed. Zach was tackling his breakfast with gusto, and she was sitting here and listening to her stomach growl? Not accepting Zach's check had been stupid enough, but wasting perfectly good food was even worse.

She scowled, reached for her fork and dug in.

When she had finished, she took a final sip of coffee, wiped her lips with a paper napkin and sat forward.

"Well?" she said brusquely. "What's this all about?"

Zach pushed away the tray, propped his elbows on the table and locked his fingers together beneath his chin.

"The past week's been—I guess the word I'm looking for is interesting."

She gave him a honeyed smile. "How fortunate for you."

Zach sighed. "Maybe what I really mean is that it's been difficult."

"Difficult?" She laughed. "How could anything be difficult for the man who knows everything?"

"We finished *The Ghost Stallion*."

Eve's left eyebrow rose. "How nice," she said politely.

"And we're about to begin *Hollywood Wedding*."

"Wonderful."

"And..." He stopped and looked at her. Her eyes were very bright, and fixed on his with rapt attention that he hoped meant her sarcasm was a lie. "And I find myself in difficulty."

"There's that word again. But what has it to do with me?"

Zach felt a muscle twitch in his jaw. She had to know where this was heading. Was she going to make him crawl?

"It has everything to do with you," he said tightly. "I have a script, a crew, a cast——"

"But?"

"But," he said grimly, "I don't have a male lead. Or a location."

So, that was why he'd asked for this meeting. Eve felt a twinge of disappointment, but that was silly. What more had she expected? As for the information he needed—why keep it from him? She'd be happy enough to see the mighty Zach Landon fail, but that would mean *Hollywood Wedding* would fail, too. And, no matter what happened, in her heart the film would always be hers.

"Dex Burton," she said. "He's right for the part."

Zach's expression darkened. "Of course. And the location?"

"In the mountains. There's this cabin I know—I can get you a map of it, if you like. I spent a weekend there, a long time ago, and——"

A weekend. With who? With a man who'd feasted on that perfect mouth, who'd learned every inch of that beautiful body?

"...finished?"

Zach blinked. "What?"

"I said, are we finished?" She rose from the bench and smiled brightly. "If we are, thank you for breakfast, but I've got to get going. I've got appointments and interviews lined up all day, and——"

"Eve." Zach stood up and came around the table toward her. "I want you to come back to Triad."

For a second, her heart soared, but then reality set in.

"We already tried that. And it was a complete flop."

"Because we let our relationship get off track, but it won't happen again. There's nothing personal in this offer, Eve," he said, hoping to God it was the truth. "My only interest is in saving Triad, and I need your help to do it."

"No."

Zach's mouth twisted under a cool smile. "Are you saying you can't work with me in a purely business relationship?"

"I'm saying I'd rather not have any kind of relationship with you."

"Because you can't handle it?"

Was he right? No. The very thought was...

"Ridiculous," she said sharply.

Zach's eyes darkened. "Is it ridiculous?"

"Stop it," she said through her teeth. "If you think I'm going to rise to some silly taunt——"

"What are you running from, Eve? Are you afraid you'll fail at Triad?" That little, infuriating smile played over his lips again. "Or that you'll end up in my bed?"

Color swept into her cheeks. "Believe me," she said coldly, "there's nothing to be afraid of!"

Zach grinned. "Was that a yes?"

Eve looked at his handsome, insolent face and lifted her chin.

"That's what it was," she snapped, and almost as soon as the foolish words were out of her mouth, she knew she'd end up regretting them.

CHAPTER SEVEN

IT BEGAN as an armed truce, with both sides civil but cautious.

Zach offered Eve a ride to work, but she declined.

"I'll meet you at the office," she said politely.

He nodded, they shook hands, and she turned away and walked to her apartment. Once inside, she leaned back against the door and told herself that the electric charge that had seemed to pass between their clasped hands had been an illusion.

What else could it have been? she thought, frowning.

She gave herself a brisk shake and headed for the bedroom to change her clothes.

Zach thought about the same thing as he drove to the office. Eve had put her hand in his, and something had flowed between them.

It had probably been static electricity, he thought, frowning as he pulled into the parking lot and got out of the Porsche. After all, static electricity could be generated just walking across a carpet.

But he and Eve had been standing in the middle of the sidewalk.

He gave himself a brisk shake as he unlocked the office door. It was just one of those scientific curiosities, then. Nothing worth thinking about. He had a lot to do this morning. It was still early—neither Emma nor Eve would be in for more than an hour.

Zach tossed his attaché case on Emma's desk, dumped his jacket on the back of her chair and rolled up his shirt sleeves. He walked quickly down the corridor to Eve's office, opened the door and switched on the light. Frowning with concentration, he looked around the room.

It would work. Yes, it would work fine, he thought, as he began emptying the drawers from Eve's desk. He paused. Maybe he should have checked with her first....

"Don't be silly," he muttered, and went on with what he was doing. "Who's the boss here, anyway?"

His work had him so absorbed that he didn't realize Eve had come into the room until he heard her startled gasp behind him. He straightened, glanced at his watch and turned around.

"You're early," he said. "I thought I'd have all this done before you got in."

Eve was all business, both in demeanor and in looks. Her hair was pulled back, her suit was tailored, her perfume was light and about as sexy as a spring shower.

And yet, her presence seemed to warm the room.

"What is all this?" she said in a baffled voice.

Zach cleared his throat and glanced around him. He wasn't finished yet, but he was getting close. He had shoved Eve's desk to the window, her file cabinets to the far wall, next to the new pair he'd ordered. A new desk, complete with telephone and fax machine, faced Eve's. All that was left was to make some sort of arrangement out of the love seat, coffee table and small bookcase in the near corner.

He smiled, started to dust his hands off on the seat of his pants, thought better of it and reached for a towel he'd liberated from the adjoining bathroom instead.

"Well? What do you think?"

Eve shook her head. "I don't know what I think, Zach. What's happened to my office?"

"Our office." He tossed the towel onto the new desk and smiled at her. "A little cramped, but not bad, huh?"

"You mean . . . you mean, we're going to share this room?"

"Well, I don't see that we have much choice. The only alternative would have been to rent space elsewhere, and then we'd spend all our time either on the phone or the fax machine. Watch it, Eve, will you? There's a deliveryman just behind you."

She stepped aside quickly, just in time for a man wheeling a box-laden dolly to come through the door. "Computer," she read silently, "monitor, printer . . ."

"You want I should set this up, mister?"

Eve swung around. Zach was scribbling his name on the delivery invoice.

"No, that's fine." He smiled as he handed the invoice over. "I can take care of it."

"Terrific." The deliveryman handed Zach one piece of paper, pocketed the other, tipped an imaginary hat to Eve and strolled from the room.

"I figured we can both use this computer," Zach said as he began opening the first box. "I would have bought two, but considering that we're cramped for space—to say nothing of money——"

"Zach." Eve licked her lips. "We can't both work in this one office."

He straightened up, put his hands on his hips and fixed her with that inflexible stare she was coming to know so well.

"Why not?"

"Well, because—because..."

Because it would be impossible to get any work done, that was why not. How would she sit here all day, every day, watching as the light gilded Zach's hair with gold, the way it was doing now? What if he made a habit of working with his jacket off and his shirt sleeves rolled up, so that she'd only have to look up from her desk and see the way his shoulders moved beneath his shirt, or the hard musculature in his forearms?

Eve took a steadying breath. "Because it's too cramped in here," she said briskly. She turned away from him, walked to her desk and tossed her briefcase on the blotter. "Look, I'd already thought about this. I knew we'd need more office space."

"And?"

"And it's not a problem. There's an old desk in the basement storeroom. I'll have the porter bring it up."

"I've already got a desk," Zach said with a little smile. "And everything else I need. Turns out there's an office equipment rental store just off Wilshire that's open from six in the morning until——"

"Not for you, Zach. For me. There's room in the reception area, if we just shift Emma a little toward the door. As soon as she gets here, I'll——"

"Don't be silly, Eve. I've no intention of displacing you. Besides, Triad's producer shouldn't be stuck out in the reception area."

"But—but..."

"Listen, I've worked in tighter spots than this." He shot her a disarming smile as he drew his chair out from his desk. "When I was in the Corps——"

"The Corps?" she said blankly.

"The Marine Corps." He sat down in the chair and leaned back. "One time I ended up in an O.P.—an observation post," he said, when her eyebrows rose. "It was a hole barely big enough for a flea and me."

"You? In the Marines?"

Zach nodded. "Yeah. Me. Why do you sound so shocked?"

"Well, I—I just..." Eve sank down in her chair. "I'm having a hard time imagining you taking orders from—what do they call them? Drill instructors?"

Zach laughed and ran his fingers through his hair. "You've seen too many movies. DIs aren't so bad." His smile tilted. "Besides, taking orders turned out to be just what I needed. The old man had tried making me understand that his way, but..."

He fell silent. What was he doing, talking about himself and the old man? The boy he'd been and the long, hard path that had brought him to manhood were of no interest to anyone but him; hadn't his ex-wife made that clear?

"Yes," Eve said, "I can imagine."

Zach looked at her. She was very still. Only her eyes moved, in a steady sweep of his face.

"I suppose he could have been a difficult man to live with," she said in a steady voice. "But I grew up without any father. Maybe that's why I was more forgiving when Charles came along and tried to take charge of my life."

"Eve. Listen, you don't owe me any explanations."

"I know that, Zach. But I think we'll work a lot better together if we clear the air." She hesitated, then gave him a faint smile. "Some of the—the difficulty between us might even be my fault, I suppose. I tend to, well, overreact when I think I'm being accused of having traded on my looks. Anyway, it's not a long story, I promise." She took a breath. "Your father and Howard Tolland, the man who used to own Triad, were friends."

"I know that."

"Howard was from the old school. He'd never quite figured out that times had changed, that movies audiences have changed——"

"Which is why he produced *The Ghost Stallion*."

A faint smile flickered over her lips. "Exactly. I was his secretary, but because he gave me more and more responsibility"

"You began to know as much about Triad as he did."

"More." She shrugged. "I'm not boasting, Zach, I just did. Howard was stuck in a time when the big studios ran Hollywood. I'd been out here long enough to know that it was the deal makers who run things now. Howard refused to see my position—we used to argue about it all the time."

"And one of those times, my father was present?"

"Yes. I had no idea Charles was thinking of buying Triad, I just thought Howard was going to ask him to invest in a project. Charles asked a lot of questions. Hard questions. Howard kept giving me signals to back off, but I wouldn't."

Zach smiled. "No. You wouldn't."

"The next thing I knew, Charles was Triad's new owner. He asked me to have dinner with him so we could discuss business." She shook her head. "I thought he was going to tell me I was fired—you know, the new broom sweeping clean, but——"

"But he offered you the chance to head Triad instead."

"Yes." Eve's eyes met his. He could see the touch of defiance in their blue depths, and in the lift of her chin. "It's not a woman's fault if some men are fool enough to fall all over themselves at the sight of a pretty face, but your father wasn't one of them."

Zach smiled. "A beautiful face," he said.

"What?"

"You're not pretty, Eve. You're beautiful. And you're right. My old man never let anything but the bottom line affect his judgment. He'd have made Horace the Wonder Horse head of Triad, if he'd thought it was the right way to go." His smile faded. "Look, this is my fault. I read the files, I did some checking up——"

"On me," Eve said flatly.

He nodded. "Yes. And—and I came up with the wrong answers."

For a minute, he almost told her that it was a lot more than that, that he'd been married to a woman who was an expert at trading for favors...

But Eve was smiling at him in a way she never had before, with a little crinkle to her nose and a sweet curve to her lips, and the sight was enough to send all the dark, angry memories of his ex-wife skittering into the shadows.

"Horace the Wonder Horse, hmm?"

Zach chuckled. "Yeah. We can always put him in to replace us both if *Hollywood Wedding* flops."

"Well, then." Eve's smile faded. "Have we settled this, Zach? Because I promise, I'm never going to defend myself to you again."

"You won't have to."

"Good." She stood, stepped back and pushed her hair away from her face. "Now, I'm going to get to work. I've got to set up an appointment with Dex Burton's agent. It won't be easy, convincing Dex to take this part, but if I can just get his agent to agree to hear me out——"

"Why?" Zach frowned. "It's a good part. Even I can tell that, just by reading the script."

"Sure it is. But Dex is just turning the corner in his career. He's probably looking to take a safe, high-profile role in a megabucks picture for somebody like Spielberg or Disney, and here we come, asking him to play a bad guy in a low-budget movie."

"A bad guy turned good guy," Zach said. "An antihero. And playing against type is good for an actor. It stretches his talent."

Eve leaned back against her desk, folded her arms and chuckled.

"I'm impressed, Mr. Landon. You've been doing your homework." She sighed. "But Dex's agent won't want to see it that way. I'll try to get him to agree to take a meeting on Monday, and then I'll FedEx the script to him."

"And then?"

"And then?" she said, puzzled.

"Yes. What's on the agenda after that?"

"Well, I'm not sure. I need to check out some copyright information on a couple of songs we're going to use in that bar scene, and then I want to go over some details about costumes, and——"

"What about checking out a place for the location shots?"

Eve chewed on her bottom lip. "You're right. I should take care of that next. I told you I've got a place in mind, didn't I?"

Zach nodded. "A cabin, you said."

"Yes. A couple of hours into the hills."

"I'd like to see it," he said thoughtfully. "It's not that I don't trust your judgment, Eve, but as executive producer——"

"Oh, of course. I wouldn't expect to do something like that on my own. I don't even know how much it will cost to rent the place. I spent the weekend there, but it was my friend who'd made all the arrangements."

Zach felt an unexpected coldness form in his belly, but he smiled pleasantly.

"I see."

"Plus, we'd have to truck in everything. The cast, the crew——"

"I suggest I take a look at this cabin before we make any further plans."

"Fine." Eve drew the telephone toward her. "I'll call Burton's agent, and then I'll contact a couple of realtors. Somebody's bound to have some information."

Zach nodded. He walked to his desk, sat down and pulled his attaché case toward him.

"Good," he said briskly. "Do whatever it takes to get the keys for a day."

"Uh-huh."

"Tomorrow would be a good time," Zach said, frowning as he took some papers from the attaché case. "It's a Saturday, so it won't interfere with work."

"Fine."

He took a breath. "That is, if you haven't already made plans for tomorrow?" he said, and looked at her.

Eve stared at him. "You want me to go with you?"

"Of course. What's the point of me going alone?"

He was right, she thought. He would have final approval, but the concept and setting for *Hollywood Wedding* were hers.

And yet, the thought of spending the day with him, the entire day, on the top of a mountain that might as well be a million miles from reality was—it was...

"Eve?"

She looked up. Zach's face was expressionless.

"Have you made other plans for tomorrow?"

She swallowed hard. "No, no, I haven't."

"Good." He nodded briskly and picked up a pencil. "In that case, I'll pick you up at seven. Okay?"

He waited for her answer, damned near holding his breath as he did. It was ridiculous to feel this way. They were going to spend the day together, but so what? He could handle that.

"Okay," Eve said at last. What did she have to be afraid of? She could handle this.

Zach nodded and bent over the string of numbers before him.

"Tomorrow, then," he said, and spent the rest of the morning pretending that he hadn't conned her into agreeing to spend the day with him—and that he had at least some faint idea of what in hell the blur of numbers on the page in front of him was supposed to mean.

She was waiting outside on the sidewalk when he drove up the next morning.

She was dressed all in white, from her cotton shirt to her slacks to her sneakers; her golden hair was pulled back from her face and held in place by a white ribbon.

How could a woman look more beautiful each time you saw her?

"Hi," she said, smiling as she climbed into the Porsche and settled into the seat beside him.

"Hi, yourself." Zach smiled back at her. "Got the keys?"

Eve nodded. "Keys," she said, plucking a skeleton key from her shoulder purse, "and a map. We're all set."

He nodded, shifted gears and moved out into the road. "Good."

"The realtor said the trip should take about two hours, maybe a little more, depending on the road."

Zach glanced in the rearview mirror. "Traffic should be fairly light, for another hour or so, anyway."

"She was talking about the road from the highway to the cabin. It's pretty narrow, as I recall, and its got more twists and turns than a snake, and——"

"You remember this place pretty clearly, don't you?"

Eve looked across the console. Was there an edge in Zach's voice? No. It had to be her imagination. He was looking at the road, smiling just a bit, the picture of relaxation in his white cotton pullover sweater and faded jeans.

It had to be her, reacting to her own nervousness.

"Yes," she said, "I suppose I do. The weekend I spent here was so terrific and such a surprise that——"

"Why don't you take a look at that map, Eve? Plot us a way out of the city along some alternate route. I was wrong about traffic being light this morning. It's starting to build already."

There wasn't much traffic, not that she could see, but Eve nodded.

"No problem. Just give me a minute."

Zach watched as she spread the map open in her lap and bent over it, her bright hair falling over her face. She lifted her hand, tucked the strands behind her ear, and as she did, the cap sleeve of her shirt rode up, exposing the pale, golden skin of her underarm.

For some foolish reason, the sight made his throat constrict with an almost unbearable tenderness.

What was wrong with him this morning? He'd been seesawing back and forth since he'd awakened, one minute whistling like a schoolboy at the long day that lay ahead with Eve, the next wondering what in hell he was so happy about. This was a Saturday, sure, but it was just an extension of the work week.

Besides, only a fool would be happy to take a woman to a place that obviously held such sweet memories for her.

Why in hell had he ever agreed to this trip?

Zach scowled at the road ahead. Not that Eve's memories mattered, one way or the other. What she'd done before she met him was her business. What she did afterward was her affair, too. Eve was stunning, and there was no denying the strong physical attraction between them, but he had no claim to her.

And he didn't want any. The last thing he wanted was to get involved again. He'd had the moonlight and roses and the promises-of-forever routine—and look where it had landed him.

"Here we go." Eve looked up from the map. "If you take the next off ramp——"

"Never mind," Zach said briskly. "You were right. We'll stay where we are—the traffic's not bad at all." He cleared his throat. "So, how'd it go with Burton?"

Eve made a face. "His agent's a jerk. He says he's too busy to meet with me next week, but he finally agreed to look at a script. So I sent him one, and sent one to Dex, too, along with a note."

"Is that what the note says?" Zach grinned. "Dear Dex, your agent's a jerk. Best wishes, Eve Palmer?"

She laughed and lay her head back. "I only wish! No, I was the soul of diplomacy. You know, I told him what a terrific actor he was, and how I'd love to see him in this role, blah, blah, blah." She sighed. "I stroked his ego until it made me want to gag, but who knows if it was enough?"

The thought of her stroking any part of Dex Burton, even his ego, made Zach's hands tighten on the wheel.

"Listen," he said, "I can always call Burton instead of you getting stuck with it."

"Thanks, but I don't think you could convince him." Zach looked over just in time to see that familiar lifting of her chin. "But I can do it," she said, "and I will."

"Well, let's not worry about that today. Tell me more about this cabin. How far off the beaten track is it?"

"Far enough. Most of the trip's not bad, but you end up on a road that winds up the mountain. Rocks on one side, vertigo on the other."

"Not your cup of tea?"

She laughed. "I learned to drive in Minnesota," she said, "where the word 'flat' was defined."

Zach laughed, too. "Well, you're in good hands. I learned to drive in the Rockies. In a car very much like this one, come to think of it."

Eve turned her head toward him. "Nice."

"Oh, yeah." A grin tilted across his mouth. "Especially since it was the old man's, and he didn't know a thing about it."

"What do you mean?"

He shrugged his shoulders. "He had a Porsche that spent its life in the garage. Well, heck, that seemed an awful waste, so I swiped his keys, had a duplicate set made and took off."

"And?"

He sighed. "And, he had me brought back."

"Cured you of borrowing what wasn't yours, huh?"

"No." He shot her a grin. "Just made me more careful about getting caught."

Eve laughed, and then she sighed and shifted into the corner of the seat.

"You said you have brothers?"

"Yeah. And a sister."

She smiled wistfully. "It must have been fun, growing up with other kids."

"Were you an only child?"

She hesitated. She never talked about her childhood. It was too painful and too revealing.

"I don't know what I was," she said, after a minute. "My mother left me on somebody's front porch with a note that said she hoped I'd get a good home."

Zach reached out and took her hand in his. "I'm sorry, Eve."

"Don't be. It was a long time ago."

"What happened? Were you adopted?"

Eve shook her head. "I went into foster care. By the time the courts decided if I could be adopted—if I'd really been abandoned or not—I was too old for anybody to want me." She smiled. "And too gawky."

"You?" His hand tightened on hers. "Gawky? I doubt that."

"Trust me," she said, with a little laugh. "I was spindly, like a colt, and just about as awkward."

He smiled at her. "But you didn't stay that way."

"No." She smiled, too, but the smile quickly faded from her face. "No, I didn't. By the time I was in my mid teens, I'd—I'd begun to mature. I was in another foster home by then, and..."

"And?" Zach said gently.

Eve hesitated. Tell him, she thought. Tell him why you could never have done the things he accused you of. Tell him how baffled you've always been by desire....

But it was too much to say, and too soon to say it. Instead, she smiled and shrugged her shoulders.

"And," she said, "I wasn't happy. So I saved up the money I earned baby-sitting, slipped out of the house one night and never looked back."

Zach's fingers curled through hers.

"I wish I'd met you then," he said gruffly. "I'd have done my damnedest to have made you happy."

You are making me happy.

The realization was swift and stunning, and for an instant, she was afraid she'd said the words out loud.

But she only smiled, and squeezed his hand tightly, and when he felt the press of her fingers and saw the muscles in her throat work, Zach felt as if she'd reached straight into his chest and wrapped her fingers around his heart.

CHAPTER EIGHT

By the time they reached the turnoff that led to the cabin, clouds had turned the sunny morning almost as dark as Zach's mood.

The closer they got to their destination, the sorrier he was he'd come.

Mud from the unseasonal rains that had hit these mountains recently had turned the road into a miserable, slippery track with enough holes to make him glad the Porsche had such responsive steering. The mountain was on his right, a drop-off to nowhere was on his left, and parts of the shoulder had given up completely and slid down the steep incline.

Why would he even consider paying what it would cost to transport a cast and crew and equipment one hundred and fifty plus miles up a mountain?

Why would he want to shoot a film in the middle of nowhere?

But mostly, he kept wondering why he'd ever agreed to bring Eve to a place where she'd spent a weekend with another man.

There was no sense kidding himself. He'd thought—he'd hoped—that this day would turn out to be pleasant and relaxing, and that it would mark a turning point in their relationship.

But it wasn't working out like that. Instead, he was sitting here feeling sorry for himself, trying not to be jealous of some faceless guy who'd once brought Eve up this same road.

And he had no right to be jealous. He'd meant it when he'd told Eve their relationship was going to be strictly business.

Okay. Zach's jaw knotted. Okay, so maybe he never should have made that promise. Maybe, deep in his gut, he'd known he wanted a more personal relationship with her after all.

So what? That still didn't give him the right to give a damn about some lover she'd had long before she met him.

He'd had more than his fair share of relationships with women over the years, both before his marriage and certainly after. He expected his women to be faithful for as long as an affair lasted, but he'd never given a damn about their pasts.

And yet here he was, thinking about the last time Eve had come up this road, wondering if she still thought about the guy who'd brought her, if her pleasant memories of the cabin were linked to the man or the place.

"Idiot," he muttered.

"What?"

Zach glanced at Eve, swallowed dryly and looked at the road.

"I said...ah, I said, I wonder what idiot designed this road?"

Eve shifted into the corner and turned toward him.

"You, too? I've been thinking that for the longest time, but I didn't want to say anything." She gave a little laugh. "I didn't want to do anything to distract you. I mean, I could see how hard you were concentrating."

Zach laughed, too. If only she knew what he'd been concentrating on, that she was the greatest distraction he could imagine.

"Zach? Do you think maybe we ought to turn back?"

"Yeah," he said dryly, "oh, yeah, I sure do. But I haven't seen a strip of road wide enough to turn a bike around, much less a car."

"Well, for whatever it's worth, I'm sorry I dragged you up here. If I'd known——"

"Come on, don't be silly. You had no way of knowing this road would give the Baja a run for its money."

He glanced at her, for the first time seeing the tilt of that resolute chin, and he could have cursed himself for his selfishness. Wrapped up in his own stupid thoughts, he'd never stopped to think how Eve might feel about finding herself on a narrow ribbon of washed-out gravel perched a few hundred feet in the air in a Porsche that might just be going faster than it should.

Zach eased his foot off the gas pedal.

"Not that I've driven the Baja," he said, flashing her a quick smile, "but I have put in time on some tracks that are every bit as miserable as this one."

It was an immodest boast, but he told himself he was only doing it to take Eve's mind off things. And it worked. She turned toward him, head cocked and eyes wide.

"You mean, you drive racing cars?"

He shrugged his shoulders. "Strictly amateur stuff, of course."

She laughed and lay her head back against the seat.

"And to think I was ready to write you off as a bean counter."

Zach grinned. "Never underestimate the bean counters of the world."

"No. I can see that. How on earth did you get into racing?"

"Well, I've always liked cars."

Eve raised an eyebrow. She reached out and patted the leather dashboard of the Porsche.

"Do tell," she said wryly. "I thought Hertz rented Porsches to everybody."

He chuckled. "Not exactly. But I've been a pretty good customer at my local dealership back East, so when I asked the manager to contact somebody out here and arrange a rental for me..."

"Couldn't do without it, hmm?"

"I admit, I like fast cars. And racing. I even thought of turning pro once."

"Why didn't you?"

"Well, it's an expensive sport and I just didn't have the money. I was just out of the Corps, going to college, and——"

"Let me guess," Eve said with a little laugh. "You paid your own way through college."

Zach nodded. "The old man and I were barely on speaking terms. He didn't offer and even if he had, I wouldn't have let him." He shot her another quick smile. "The Corps taught me the importance of honor, integrity, independence—and that only a sucker thinks he's going to fill an inside straight."

The road angled into the trees, and Zach almost breathed a sigh of relief. The surface was even muddier, but at least they'd left the edge of the world behind.

"I agree," Eve said. "About it being important to be independent." Her smile tilted. "I've always had this little scenario in my head. About my mother, you know? How she must have been young, and dependent on her family, and how different her life and mine would have been if—if…"

She fell silent. She was doing it again, telling him things about herself she'd never told anyone. It was pointless, this—this giving away of little pieces of herself. And why would Zach want to hear these foolish confessions, anyway?

His hand closed around hers. "Listen," he said gruffly, "if success is a path to independence, you'll have plenty of it once *Hollywood Wedding* hits the theaters."

Eve's fingers tightened around his. "I hope so. But there are still so many loose ends.…" She drew in her breath, then expelled it. "And I know I've made mistakes. Thinking we could use this cabin for a location, for instance—I must have been out of my mind."

"Don't tell me you're starting to question all those great memories of the place?" he said in what he hoped was a light tone.

"No, not at all. But this road…we'd never be able to get anything up here, except by helicopter. And…" She leaned forward. "Look," she said, "there it is. See? Just through the trees."

The cabin stood in a small clearing, surrounded by the lush green of the forest. Zach pulled the car up beside it and shut off the engine. Somewhere off in the distance, thunder rolled softly across the mountain.

Eve swung toward him, her eyes bright. "You can see why I thought it would be perfect, can't you?"

Zach felt his gut knot. What he could see was that this was the perfect place for a man and a woman to spend a weekend away from the world.

He shrugged, undid his seat belt and stepped out of the car.

"I'll reserve judgment until I get a look inside."

A heavy planked door swung open into a large, attractive, wood-planked room. A long, low sofa draped with a colorful afghan stood before a massive stone fireplace that dominated one wall. To the right was a small kitchen and beyond, through a partly open door, Zach could glimpse an enormous redwood hot tub set beneath a round skylight.

And to the left, within a sleeping area screened by a half-wall, there was a quilt-covered bed, a bed that looked as wide and soft as a cloud.

"I was right," Eve said softly, "it *is* perfect."

Perfect. The knot in Zach's belly grew tighter. Perfect for the film—and for bringing that sweetly nostalgic smile to her face.

"Zach?" Eve swung toward him. "What would it cost to helicopter everything up here? We'll only have a two-person cast for these shots, and——"

"Forget about it."

"Of course. You're right. It would be foolish to spend so much money."

"Exactly." Zach took her arm. "Let's go."

"Wait a minute!" She pulled away from him and walked to the center of the room. "I've got an idea."

Zach stuffed his hands into the pockets of his jeans. "Eve, it's a long drive down. And I didn't much like the looks of that sky, so if it's all the same to you——"

"I know it wouldn't be the same as using the cabin itself," she said, "but what if we come back with a camera? Take some shots, some measurements..."

"What for?"

"We could build a set duplicating the cabin on a sound stage." She smiled. "How's that sound?"

"Forget it. I wouldn't use this place if we could walk our stuff up here."

Her face fell. "You don't like it?"

"No," he said grimly, "I do not."

"Zach, come on. Remember the script?" She smiled as she walked toward him and put her hand lightly on his arm. "Think about that big love scene, you know the one, where the main characters realize their anger has just been a cover-up for their real feelings." Her fingers curled around his arm; he could feel the heat of them burning through his sleeve. "Can't you just see it? The fire in the hearth, the flames casting shadows over them...."

Thunder rolled in the distance.

"Time to go," Zach said briskly, and turned toward the door.

"Dammit, Zach." Eve stepped around him, blocking his way, her hands on her hips. "Why are you being so stubborn? Use a little imagination here, okay?"

"What we need is some practicality. You think this place is some kind of Shangri-La. I don't."

Her chin lifted. "Just tell me what's wrong with it."

It's full of ghosts, he wanted to say, *and it drives me crazy to think of you with somebody else.*

"Well?" Eve folded her arms. "Tell me one thing that's wrong with my cabin."

Zach looked at her. "I don't have to. Final decisions are mine."

"And creative ones are mine."

"Subject to my approval," he said coolly.

He could see the rapid rise and fall of her breasts, the splashes of color across her cheeks. She was angry and defiant, and it only made her more beautiful.

Zach felt his throat constrict. He didn't want to quarrel with her. He wanted to take her in his arms, kiss her until she trembled, exorcise the ghosts that haunted this cabin—that haunted him—by making love to her. Wildly. Tenderly. Passionately—until she clung to him and sighed his name.

"Okay, Zach." Her chin lifted even farther. "Do your thing. Be pigheaded and dictatorial, but I'm telling you, you're making a mistake."

Pigheaded? Hell. That was him, all right. He *was* making a mistake, and it was time to do something about it, to reach out and take her in his arms.

"Eve," he said, and took a step forward.

But she was already swinging away from him. "If you knew anything about movies," she said, yanking the door open, "you'd realize that *Hollywood Wedding* is a woman's film. I was up here with three women, Zach, three perfectly normal, average American women. And every last one of us thought this was just about the most romantic place we'd ever seen."

He stood there, his jaw dropping, as she marched toward the car.

Three women? She'd been here with three *women?*

"Three women?" He said the words stupidly as he went after her, caught her and spun her toward him.

"So what?"

"Well—well..."

Well, what, Landon? What can you say that won't make you sound like an ass?

He cleared his throat. "Well, what you just said makes sense. About this being a woman's film, I mean. And if—if the women you were with all gave this cabin points for being perfect, who am I to knock it?"

He held his breath while she glared at him. God, but he felt dumb, not just for the way he'd been behaving but for what he was doing now, lying like a kid caught with his hand in the cookie jar.

But he couldn't let her know the truth, that thinking of her belonging to any man but him was more than he could stand, that something was happening to him, something he wasn't ready for.

"Well, then," she said, and very slowly a smile edged across her lips. "There's hope for you yet, Mr. Landon."

Zach smiled back at her. "Yeah. I think maybe there is."

"Amy, Beth, Susie and I all loved it here."

"The Little Women's vote of approval," he said, and laughed because otherwise he was going to say to hell with it and sweep her into his arms.

Her smile became a grin. "Exactly. I mean, we didn't know what to expect. Amy's brother had rented the place for the weekend. He was going to bring his girlfriend here and propose, but she came down with the flu or something. So he told Amy she could have the place, and she invited the rest of us. We all waited tables together at..."

She went on talking, telling him about their weekend, how they'd driven up here not knowing what to expect and how much fun they'd had doing kid stuff, hiking the woods and toasting marshmallows and singing around the fire at night.

And Zach nodded and smiled when she smiled, and he knew that whatever happened all the rest of his life, he would always remember this moment, when he'd first realized that he was—that he was...

"Eve?" he whispered, and she stopped in the middle of a sentence and looked at him. He saw the bloom of color sweep into her cheeks, heard the sharp intake of her breath, and then she was in his arms.

Thunder rumbled across the clearing, a sound that seemed no louder or deeper than the thud of his heart. Lightning lit the sky, but it barely registered against his closed eyelids.

And then the sky tore apart.

Eve shrieked as a silver curtain of rain spilled from the sky. She pulled back in Zach's arms, her hair already soaked, her clothing drenched.

They looked at each other and began to laugh.

Zach scooped her into his arms.

"I think it's raining," he shouted, above the roar of the storm.

She looped her arms around his neck. "We should have brought a bar of soap," she shouted back.

He trotted across the clearing and into the cabin, shouldering the door closed behind him.

"My God, woman," he said, "you look like you've been into that hot tub with all your clothes on!"

Eve laughed. "So do you."

Zach's smile faded, becoming something sexy and dangerous.

"It seems to me," he said softly, "that we're going to have to get out of these wet clothes."

Eve's heart skipped a beat. "Zach," she whispered, "Zach, listen..."

He bent his head and kissed her. It was a long, gentle kiss, and as it went on, as it changed and became hot with need and electric with desire, Eve knew it was time to admit the truth.

Somewhere between that dusty hillside where Zach had almost run over Horace the Wonder Horse and this isolated cabin, somewhere during all the quarrels and anger, she had fallen hopelessly, desperately in love.

Her lips parted, opened to his. Her hands clung to his broad shoulders.

"Zach," she whispered against his mouth, and the single word said everything he needed to hear.

He lowered her to her feet, cupped her face in his hands. His fingers swept into her hair and fisted in its rich, silken strands. He tipped her head back and kissed her again, his teeth nipping at her soft bottom lip, his tongue slipping against hers like hot silk.

"I've dreamed about this," he whispered. "About holding you in my arms and kissing you."

Eve pulled his head down to hers. "Kiss me, then," she said fiercely. "Kiss me, and never stop."

His fingers dropped to the buttons that ran the length of her cotton shirt, and he undid them slowly. She was wearing a silky bra beneath the shirt, something pink and lacy that had a front clasp. His fingers trembled as he opened it, and his heart turned over.

She was so beautiful.

"Beautiful," he whispered. "My Eve."

His hands dropped to her belt. Her eyes flew open as he undid it, then her zipper.

"Eve," he said, and there was a tremor in his voice.

"Yes," she whispered, hearing the question, knowing she could give only one answer. "Yes," she sighed as the rest of her clothing fell away from her, and she stood, for the first time in her life, naked to a man's gaze.

Zach looked at her and wondered how any woman could be so lovely. Her breasts were round as apples, ivory colored and tipped with nipples as pink as furled rosebuds. She had a waist he could almost span with his hands, a sweetly curved belly that tapered into golden curls, softly rounded hips and long, long legs.

"My beautiful Eve," he whispered.

He looked into her face. It was flushed with color, and her eyes were wide and filled with expectancy.

"I—I want to see you, too," she said.

He smiled. "Undress me, then."

The color in her face darkened. She hesitated, and then she stepped closer and lay her hands against his chest. Her palms felt like fire, burning through his wet shirt.

"Lift your arms," she whispered.

Slowly, she eased the shirt over his head, catching her breath when she saw the hard musculature in his arms and shoulders, the soft, dark curls that laced across his chest.

Her gaze dropped lower, to his ridged abdomen, to his navel, to the belt looped through his jeans.

Blood pounded in her temples as she reached out and undid the belt. Her hands were shaking; she managed to undo the button at the top of his fly but when she reached for the zipper tab, she faltered.

Zach caught her hand in his. "I'll do it," he said huskily, afraid of what might happen to him if he felt even the softest touch of her hand.

She nodded and stepped back, waiting.

And then he was naked, too, that powerful, masculine body exposed in all its terrifying beauty.

Suddenly, Eve felt uncertain.

"Zach?" she whispered.

"Yes," he said, "oh, yes, my love..."

He gathered her to him and kissed her deeply, and as he did, he lifted her in his arms and carried her to the bed.

She fell back against the soft pillows, her eyes locked on his face as he bent to her. Her lashes fluttered to her cheeks as he kissed her mouth, her throat, and then his lips were on her breast.

Eve moaned, buried her fingers in his hair and sighed his name.

His lips closed around her nipple and he drew the silken bead between his teeth. His hand slid over her belly, dipped into the golden curls and he drew back, burning with the need to see her face when he touched her. Slowly, slowly, he brought his fingers toward those golden curls again, feeling the tremor arcing through her muscles as he came closer. When, finally, his fingers stroked her, a moan broke from her throat.

"My Eve," he said fiercely, and found and caressed that sweetest of feminine mysteries.

She arced toward him, her hand dropping hard on his.

"Don't," she whispered, "Zach, don't. I can't bear it."

But she could. Oh, she could. She could exult in what he was making her feel, a pleasure exquisite beyond anything she'd ever imagined.

She moaned again and Zach bent and kissed her mouth, his tongue moving against hers while his fingers went on with their sweet torment.

Something was building inside her, an almost unendurable tension. She was—she was...

A cry burst from her lips as she shattered against his hand. Zach gathered her close in his arms, kissing her as she trembled against him, whispering soft, sweet words, and then, at last, he parted her thighs and knelt between them.

At the last instant, he hesitated. It was the moment he had longed for, Eve lying beneath him, her eyes on his, her lips soft and swollen from his kisses.

And yet, though he'd known how perfect this would be, it seemed to transcend perfection. There was a softness to her, a vulnerability he had never anticipated.

"Zach?" she whispered.

He looked at her, seeing the sweet curve of her mouth, the expectation in her eyes. With a groan, he cupped her bottom, lifted her to him and sheathed himself in her slick, silken heat.

His head fell back, he cried out her name, and exploded into a million shimmering fragments.

CHAPTER NINE

BY LATE afternoon, the storm was almost over. The sky began to clear, the rain fell off to a soft drizzle, and at the edge of the forest, a bird sent up a first, hesitant call.

Eve lay in Zach's arms, safe and warm and filled with a joy so fierce it was almost painful.

I love you, she thought, closing her eyes and pressing her lips to his throat, *oh, how I love you...*

"Sweetheart?"

She nodded, afraid to speak.

Zach drew her closer. "Are you all right?"

She smiled. "I'm wonderful."

Laughing softly, he turned on his side, still holding her in the curve of his arm.

"Immodest woman." He nuzzled a spill of damp, golden hair from her cheek and kissed her ear. "But it's true, you are."

Eve lifted her head, propped her chin on her hand and looked into his face.

"Well, if I am, you get half the credit."

He grinned. "Thank you."

Eve smiled, kissed him, then lay her head on his chest.

What would he say, she wondered, if she told him he got all the credit? That not only had their lovemaking been glorious but that she had never been with a man before? She knew Zach had no idea she'd been a virgin.

He had made love to her so gently, so passionately, that she'd never felt inhibited or afraid.

As for the blood and pain all the books she'd read mentioned—well, there'd been none. There'd only been sweet, sweet pleasure and the sense of being made joyously, completely whole.

Eve sighed. She knew her view of sex had been warped by the ugly memory of her foster father's attempted seduction. Still, she'd never dreamed lying in a man's arms could be so—so...

"Perfect," Zach whispered, rising above her. He smiled and kissed her, while his hand moved softly over her body.

Eve's breath caught as he bent to her breast.

"Yes," she whispered. "That's the word. Perfect."

His kisses trailed over her belly, down and down...

"Zach," she whispered, and then she could think no more.

They made an improvised meal of canned rations some prior tenant had left in the cabin, but by the time they started down the mountain the next morning, they were starved.

Zach stopped at the first restaurant they came to in the foothills and ordered an enormous brunch.

"I'll never eat all this," Eve protested, when their meal arrived. But she did. Every crumb. She laughed and said she'd never eaten so much in her life, and Zach gave her a slow, sexy smile and said he never had, either. Their eyes met, and Eve flushed with pleasure.

It was a sunny, bright day, one Zach insisted was made for the beach. Eve agreed, and they drove all the way to Venice where they strolled the boardwalk, drinking chilled cappuccino and doing their best to keep out of the way of the roller bladers. At sunset, they took off their shoes and walked hand in hand through the surf, sharing kisses that tasted of sun and of the sea.

That night, after lobsters and white wine at a restaurant in Malibu, Zach drove Eve home.

"I don't want to leave you," he whispered, after endless kisses in her darkened living room.

"I know," she sighed, leaning back in his arms. "It's been such a wonderful weekend, I don't want it to end, either."

"It doesn't have to. Let me stay with you tonight."

Eve's smile tilted. "I don't think that's a good idea."

"I think it's a great idea."

She touched her finger to his lips. "We both have to go to work tomorrow, remember?"

"Yeah, but I know your boss. He's a very understanding guy. He won't mind if you come in a little late."

"Hollywood's a small town, Zach," she said softly. "It thrives on gossip. I—I don't want to be talked about."

"Come on, Eve. This is the dawn of the twenty-first century. The sky's not going to fall down if people know we're lovers."

But the fingers would point, the whispers would start— and she had had enough of that in her life. Tell him that, she thought, tell him about your foster father, about the way the rumor mill ground out its evil stories, even here in a place some called Sin City after Charles put her in charge of Triad.

She couldn't. Not yet. Talking about those things was too painful and intimate, in some strange way even more intimate than what they'd shared in bed.

So she smiled and offered what she hoped was an explanation Zach would understand.

"I don't think it would be good for Triad if people know about us."

Zach gave a little laugh. "What the hell does Triad have to do with this?"

"Well—well, we're working on *Hollywood Wedding* together, remember? You have to deal with people, I have to deal with people. How much authority would we have if people thought they could trade on our relationship with each other? I think it would be better if people saw us as sort of separate entities. Zach?" Eve rose on her toes and kissed his mouth. "Do you understand?"

He didn't, but how could he argue with her when she was in his arms? A man would have to be a fool or a saint, and he was neither.

"No," he said, softening the word with a smile. "Not really. But if that's the way you want it..." His hands slipped to her hips and he brought her body against his. "But if being seen as separate entities means I'm going to have to take a vow of chastity," he said with a teasing laugh, "forget it."

She put her arms around his neck. "No," she whispered, "I wouldn't want that." They kissed, and then she put her hands gently against his chest. "Good night, Zach."

Zach made a sound halfway between a laugh and a groan.

"Right." He kissed her again, then let her go. At the door, he turned to her and smiled. "I'll see you in the morning."

Eve smiled at him. "Bright and early."

But not bright and early enough, he thought as he headed for his car. He'd wanted to fall asleep with Eve in his arms, wake her with his kisses.

Didn't she want the same thing?

Frowning, he got behind the wheel and drove off.

They plunged into work on *Hollywood Wedding* with renewed vigor. All the final details began falling into place.

Zach met again with Ed Brubeck, who said he'd be happy to do what he could, now that Eve was back on board. Other investors said much the same thing, and the money began to come in.

Eve arranged to have a photographer visit the cabin and take still shots. The set designer was sure he could duplicate the cabin without too much difficulty.

"Great," Eve said, and concentrated her efforts on Dex and his agent.

It wasn't easy. The agent was going to play hardball. He finally agreed that he might consider advising Dex to sign for the part, but he wanted concessions, she told Zach over a midweek lunch at one of the city's newest watering holes.

"What kinds of concessions?" Zach asked suspiciously.

Eve made a face. "Impossible ones. He hasn't put them on the table yet, but he's hinting at bonuses, final cut approval and a rewrite of the script that would all but gut it."

"Did you laugh in his face?"

She smiled. "I was a bit more diplomatic than that. I told him we might consider a percentage deal instead."

"And?"

"And," she said with a little sigh, "he said he'd think about it."

Zach picked up his coffee cup. "Maybe it's time to consider some other actor for the part."

"Not yet. We've still got some time left. Actually, I think I might be better off if I bypass Dex's agent and go straight to Dex himself."

Zach's eyes narrowed. "I don't like the guy, Eve. I'd just as soon you kept away from him."

"I don't like him, either." She looked across the table and into Zach's eyes. "You know that. But liking Dex or disliking him has nothing to do with knowing he's right for this part."

Zach's jaw tightened. "Dealing with Dex instead of his agent is just trading one jerk for another."

Eve laughed. "You're right—but it's worth a shot."

Zach nodded. She was right. His feelings about Dex were his own problem. Eve was producing this film, and signing actors was her business.

"Sure," he said. He even managed to smile. "Just keep me posted."

By Thursday, Eve had spoken with Dex on the phone several times but he still hadn't come around. In desperation, she agreed to meet him for lunch.

She arrived at the restaurant prepared for anything and found—to her relief—that Dex had turned over a new leaf.

He was charming and witty, and that was all. There were no hands moving under the table, no offers of the good time they could have if they met somewhere more private.

But there was one moment at the end of the meal....

Dex suddenly leaned over the table. "Do you seriously think I'd do this movie without some personal concessions from you, Evie?" he said softly.

Eve, who was signing their check, looked up. There was something in his voice that made the hair rise on the back of her neck. But Dex was smiling pleasantly, his expression open and easy, and she knew she was being ridiculous.

Dex was talking about business concessions, nothing more.

"We're prepared to offer you a percentage above the line, Dex," she said with a cheerful smile. "I think that's enough."

Dex laughed. "It's a concession, Evie. But hardly enough."

There it was, that same undertone.

"Okay," he said.

Eve blinked. "Okay?"

Dex grinned. "Well, I'll at least consider the offer."

The next day—Friday—Dex telephoned. He told Eve he'd thought things over and decided she might be right. Maybe it was time he took a chance on something different.

"Let's talk about it tonight, at dinner."

Eve hesitated, but what choice was there? This was Friday, and she was running out of time.

"All right," she said, trying not to sound as reluctant as she felt. "No, don't pick me up. I'll meet you at Spago's, at eight."

"Meet who at eight?" Zach said, as he came walking into the office.

"Zach," Eve said happily. She rose to her feet as he shut the door. "How'd your meeting go?"

"Terrific." He put his arms around her. "But I missed you."

"Emma's right outside," Eve whispered, but she settled into his arms.

He grinned. "Emma's not a dope. She sees the way I look at you. Now, tell me who we're meeting for dinner tonight—and why. I planned on having you to myself."

"I know. But..." She hesitated. It was foolish, but she felt as if Zach had caught her doing something she shouldn't have been. "Not us," she said. "Just me. I'm having dinner with Dex. I think he's come around."

Zach frowned. He let go of her and walked to his desk.

"Good," he said brusquely. "Tell him to have his agent give me a call."

"I said, I *think* he's come around, Zach. I'll know more after I've met with him tonight."

Zach yanked off his jacket, loosened his tie and sat down behind his desk. He pulled a stack of papers toward him and began leafing through them.

"I don't understand this town," he said tightly. "Why have offices if meetings always take place in restaurants?"

"Come on," she said gently. "You've told me yourself you do half your business on golf courses or playing racquetball."

He bent over a letter, pretending he was reading it, wishing he could deny what she'd said—but he couldn't. Almost any kind of business conversation went better outside the stuffy confines of an office. Hadn't he just talked Triad's way into a couple of million bucks worth of loans after a fast game of tennis?

He looked up. "You're right." Rising, he came around the desk and took her in his arms. "But the thought of you having dinner with that jerk..." He shook his head. "I'm irritable as a bear, sweetheart. I'm sorry. It's just that I've missed you this week."

"I've been right here all the time," she said with a little smile.

"Don't joke about it. I'm going crazy, Eve. I think this has been the longest week of my life."

A flush rose in her cheeks. She didn't have to ask what he meant. She felt the same frustration. They had not made love since they'd left the cabin.

Zach had asked her to come to his hotel, but the thought of walking past the reception desk to the bank of elevators had been daunting. He'd offered to come to her apartment, but Eve had pictured the nosy Mrs. Harmon watching through the spy hole as he arrived.

In the end, they'd made do with dinner. With walks on the beach. With going to a new, much-heralded movie. But it wasn't enough, not anywhere near enough.

"Eve." Zach took her face in his hands. "Let's go away for the weekend. Acapulco, maybe. Or San Francisco. I know a little hotel just off Russian Hill that you'll love."

She thought of everything there was to do this weekend, the appointment she'd made with the still photographer, the Sunday brunch she'd set with the actress who was to star in *Hollywood Wedding*.

She thought of all that, smiled and said, "Yes."

Zach let out his breath. For a moment there, he'd half expected her to turn him down. But that was impossible. She wanted to be alone with him as much as he wanted to be alone with her, and his arms tightened around her as he thought of what the weekend would be like.

"Will you pick me up early Saturday morning?"

He grinned. "I'll do better than that. We'll leave this afternoon, right after work. How's that?"

"Perfect. All I need is an hour to pack, and..." Eve's face fell. "Oh, Zach. I've got that dinner appointment. With Dex."

She saw the smile fade from his face.

"Dammit," he growled. "The hell with him. Break the appointment."

"No, I can't. I told you——"

"I know what you told me. And I'm telling you, the hell with Burton. Call him up, tell him to either agree to our deal or forget about it."

"Zach, please——"

"He's hitting on you, isn't he?"

Her eyes flew to Zach's face. It was as harsh and unyielding as his voice.

"Come on, Eve, I'm not a fool. The first time I met Burton, you told me you thought he was a creep. I know the reason. He's been trying to get you into bed."

Eve flushed. "Maybe, in the past. But that's all done with. I told you, he sees the potential in *Hollywood Wedding*. And——"

"Why didn't you tell me?"

"Because I'm a big girl, Zach. I can take care of myself." She put her hand on his arm. The tension in it almost thrummed beneath her fingers. "It was just a game he plays, and now it's over."

"In that case, have dinner with him." His eyes met hers. "But I'm coming along."

"Zach, don't be ridiculous. I don't need protection."

His smile was wolflike. "Humor me. If he's serious about this part, he won't mind my presence."

Dex *was* serious now, Eve was sure of it. Still, she had the feeling that bringing the two men together would be like trying to mix oil and water.

"Eve?"

She looked at Zach. He was smiling pleasantly, but she could sense the tension still smoldering in him, and she knew what she had to do.

The movie was important—but nothing could ever be as important as Zach.

She sighed and put her arms around his neck. "Whatever you say," she whispered.

Zach felt the tension ease from him as his arms went around her and he kissed her. It was a long, sweet kiss, filled with promise and tenderness, and when it ended, he knew it was time to admit the truth, to himself and to Eve.

He was head over heels in love.

This was going to be one heck of a weekend, Zach thought as he pulled the Porsche to the curb outside Eve's apartment that evening. Oh, yeah, it was going to be a winner.

He smiled as he got out of the car and trotted up the steps to the door.

I love you, Eve, he would say, in the tiny, romantic garden of the hotel in San Francisco. *I love you—and I want to marry you.*

God, he could hardly believe it. His heart surged into his throat as he rang the doorbell. He had never imagined himself falling in love again. Marrying again . . .

The door opened. Eve stood there, smiling, a vision of perfection in a short black dress, and Zach knew that he was kidding himself.

He had never been in love before, not really. And he'd never been married, either, not the way he would be, once he married Eve.

She was everything he'd ever wanted in a woman and never thought he'd find. A friend. A partner. A lover.

"Zach?" Eve gave him a searching look. "What is it? You look so strange."

He wanted to take her in his arms and kiss her. Better still, he wanted to drop to one knee and make the most old-fashioned marriage proposal a man had made since Romeo proposed to Juliet.

But not with Mrs. Harmon's eye behind the spy hole in the door. Not with Dex Burton waiting in the wings.

No. This had to be just right. Tomorrow, he thought, tomorrow...

"I was just wondering if I'd ever seen a more beautiful sight than you," he said. Eve smiled, and he put his arm around her and led her down the steps. "Good night, Mrs. Harmon," he called, waving a hand high in the air.

Eve looked at his laughing face. She laughed, too, and leaned into his shoulder.

Maybe the night wasn't going to be so difficult, after all.

Dex was a study in sophistication. If he was surprised to find Zach with Eve, he didn't show it.

"Both principals from Triad," he said. "I'm flattered."

"Eve and I are a team," Zach said with a polite smile.

But the arm he slid around Eve's waist, the way he held her against his side, said something more.

Eve saw Dex's eyebrows raise, and she stiffened. This was precisely the kind of thing she'd told Zach she wanted to avoid.

But why? She loved this man, and she was beginning to dare think he might love her, too. Her heart filled with joy at the thought. She'd been wrong, wanting to hide their relationship.

"Yes," she said, smiling at Dex, "Zach's right. We are."

"How nice for you both," Dex said pleasantly, and they settled in at the table.

The evening went well, but even after dessert and coffee, Dex still hadn't committed to the role.

"I know what you're saying, Eve. I understand this part would give me the chance to test my mettle." He sighed. "But I'm just not fully convinced."

Zach leaned forward. "What more can we offer you, Burton? Eve's outlined an excellent package. If the film does well—and we're convinced it will—you'll not only reap terrific publicity, you'll make a fortune."

Dex nodded. "I know. But, as I say, I'm not yet completely convinced."

He looked at Eve and smiled, and as he did, she felt his hand on her leg.

She froze, jerked back and shot a quick glance at Zach, but he was frowning into his coffee cup. He'd had enough of Dex's posturing, she knew, and that was a damned good thing, because all she wanted right now was to get out of here.

The slimy bastard! He hadn't finished his ugly little game yet. She could only imagine that it must give him a perverse kind of excitement, thinking he could play it in front of Zach when he knew she and Zach were lovers.

He was wrong. Dead wrong, Eve thought coldly. She would find a way to make Triad succeed without Burton, and even if it didn't, *Hollywood Wedding* was only a movie.

Zach—Zach was everything.

She shoved back her chair. "Zach," she said, "it's late."

Zach looked up. "Yes." There was surprise in his eyes, and then relief. He smiled at her as he signaled to their waiter. "It is."

"It's not late," Dex said, still smiling. "It's the shank of the evening."

"I don't think so," Eve said coolly, and stood up. "Goodbye, Dex."

Zach caught up to her as she stepped out of the restaurant.

"Hey." He turned her toward him. "Eve?" His smile was puzzled. "What happened back there?"

"Nothing much. I just decided that you were right. Dex is not only a fool, he's a sneaky little leech, as well. The one thing he isn't is the only actor in Hollywood."

Zach put his arm around her as the parking attendant hurried off to get the Porsche from the lot.

"Did I upset you? Letting him know you and I were...that we're involved. I didn't plan it, it just seemed to happen."

"I'm glad it did. I was wrong about keeping us a secret." She looked at him. "I did have reasons, Zach. And—and it's time to tell you what they are."

Zach put a finger beneath her chin, tilted her face up and kissed her gently.

"Not tonight," he said huskily. "Tomorrow, darling. When we reach San Francisco. I have something to tell you then, too." A faint smile curved across his lips. "I can't believe I'm saying this, but I'm not even going to ask you to come back to my hotel with me tonight." His smile faded. "Just tell me this. If I'd asked, would you have come?"

"Yes," she whispered. "But this is better. I can go home and make myself beautiful for you tomorrow."

Zach smiled. "You couldn't be more beautiful than you already are."

The attendant drove up in the Porsche. Zach handed the boy a tip that made his eyes bulge, and he and Eve got into the car.

Once they'd pulled out into traffic, he reached across the shift lever and took her hand in his.

Had there really been a time he had distrusted this woman? He almost laughed.

If the answer was yes, it must have been in another lifetime.

CHAPTER TEN

EVE locked the door to her apartment and leaned against it, smiling.

In all her life, she had never been this happy.

Zach had walked her to the door, taken her in his arms and given her a kiss filled with promise. When it ended, he'd framed her face in his hands.

"Eve," he'd whispered, "my beautiful Eve, I——"

Both of them had heard the sound of Mrs. Harmon's door as it eased open. Zach had groaned, laughed and planted a kiss on Eve's forehead.

"Tomorrow, darling," he'd said.

Whistling jauntily, he'd trotted down the steps.

Eve knew—oh, she knew—what he'd been going to say. The unspoken words had almost shimmered in the air.

I love you.

She did a mad, swift dance around her tiny living room. What a wonderful night this had turned out to be, she thought happily. In some strange way, she probably owed Dex a vote of thanks.

Dex. Eve shuddered. She could still see his lecherous smile, feel his oily touch.

"Ugh," she said, and began stripping off her clothes.

By the time she reached the bathroom, there was a trail of clothes behind her—her high-heeled sandals, her black dress, her stockings, her panties, her bra.

With a final shudder, she stepped into the shower.

* * *

Zach drove toward his hotel, still whistling, still feeling wonderful.

That old snoop, Mrs. Harmon. He laughed as he coasted to a stop at a red light. If she hadn't poked her nose out the door, Eve would know how he felt by now. He'd been determined to wait for tomorrow and a more romantic setting, but standing there with Eve in his arms, he'd known he had to tell her.

Those three most simple, most complex words in the world had been on the very tip of his tongue—until Mrs. Harmon had turned a twosome into a threesome.

He should have said the words anyway. To heck with Mrs. Harmon. To heck with romantic settings. What did he need but Eve and those three magic words?

Zach leaned out his window.

"I love her," he yelled to the startled driver in the next lane.

He loved her too much to wait for tomorrow.

The light went green. Zach shot a look into his rearview mirror, jammed his foot to the floor and damned near fishtailed the Porsche into a U-turn.

Eve was still in the shower. She had scrubbed the part of her thigh Dex had touched until the skin was red. She knew it was silly, but it made her feel better.

She laughed as she tilted her face to the spray. Not that she wasn't feeling wonderful already. How she loved Zach. How she adored him!

Why had she let him leave tonight? She could have asked him to come in, to stay with her for the first time in her very own bed.

Being in his arms would have erased the memory of Dex's sleazy touch better than all the soap and hot water in the world.

She stepped from the shower and wrapped herself in a towel. Her heart tripped into a quicker cadence. There was nothing to stop her from phoning Zach at his hotel.

If only he'd asked to stay. If only he'd think what she was thinking and come back . . .

The doorbell rang.

"Zach," Eve whispered.

Who else could it be, on this night of miracles?

The bell pealed again, the sound of it as impatient as the race of her pulse.

"I'm coming," Eve called, as she flew down the hall. Laughing, she slipped the bolt, undid the chain and threw the door open. "You came back," she said, "oh, my love . . ."

But it wasn't Zach at all. It was Dex.

"What a charming greeting, darling. It's always nice to find a warm welcome."

Eve's heart hammered in her throat. "Get out of here!"

"Weren't you waiting for me, darling?" He laughed, low in his throat, and fumes of whiskey inundated her as he whipped a bouquet of blood-red roses from behind his back and presented them with a flourish. "I'm the kind of man you need, Evie. I'll make you forget your Mr. Landon before the night's over."

Eve moved swiftly, throwing her shoulder against the door at the same time she tried to force it shut. Dex, half a foot taller and many pounds heavier, simply laughed, pushed past her and strolled into the living room.

Be calm, Eve told herself. Don't let him see how frightened you are.

"Dex," she said. "Dex, listen to me. Leave now, and I'll forget this happened."

"Evie, darling." She flinched as he reached past her and shut the door. "How can you say that after all the promises you've made?"

"You have a career to protect. A reputation——"

"Don't be a child, Evie. Nobody's ever going to know about this but you and me."

"I'll file charges. I'll ruin you!"

"You'll ruin yourself, you mean. Think about it, Eve. Who's more important in this town, you or me? Who's going to believe that Dex Burton would use force to get a woman?"

"Why are you doing this?" Eve whispered.

Dex's eyes turned cold with rage. "Do you have any idea how many people saw you walk out on me tonight?"

"I didn't walk out. We talked business, we finished and——"

"You got up, you and your precious Mr. Landon, and you left me standing there like a fool. Everybody who's anybody in this town saw what happened." Dex pulled off his jacket and tie and dropped them to the floor. "Your choice, Eve. We can do this the easy way or the hard way."

A sob broke from Eve's throat. She made her move, bolting past him in a desperate break for freedom, but Dex was too fast. He caught her, ripped the towel away and swung her into his arms.

"That's all right," he said. "I like it when my ladies give me a little rough and tumble."

He bent his head and kissed her. Eve slammed her fists against his shoulders but he laughed, caught her wrists in one hand and kissed her again as he carried her toward the bedroom.

She tore her hands free and hit him again, her fingers catching in his shirt and ripping it open. Dex dropped her on the bed, held her down with one hand as he shrugged off the torn shirt and undid his trousers. He fell on top of her, caught her head in his hands and held her prisoner as he kissed her.

"You son of a bitch!"

The roar of Zach's voice filled the room. Dex cried out as he was lifted bodily into the air and flung like a rag doll into the corner.

Eve scrambled to her knees. "Zach. Oh, Zach, thank God you came back. He was——"

"Give it up, Evie. Your boyfriend knows what's happening here."

Zach swung around. His adrenaline level was so high that he could barely see through the red cloud in front of his eyes. It was only seconds since he'd found Eve's door ajar. Fear had sent him racing into the apartment, but that fear had turned to blind, senseless fury when he saw the reason the door hadn't been fully closed.

Roses were scattered on a floor littered with a woman's dress and high-heeled sandals. A man's jacket and tie had been kicked into a corner. Her bra and panties, his torn shirt, made a clear trail of passion straight to this bed. To Eve, naked and flushed. To Dex Burton, on top of her...

"Zach."

He turned and looked at Eve. She had pulled the blanket around herself. Now she stood beside the bed, her eyes on his.

"He's lying," she whispered. "Zach, he was trying to—to..."

"Come on, man," Dex said. "Do I look like I need to break down doors to get what I want?" He bent down and retrieved his shirt from the floor. "The babe's been after this movie deal for weeks. Tonight, I could see she was really upset with my screwing around. So after you left, I thought, well, it's time to fish or cut bait, you know?" Dex smiled his million-dollar smile. "So I phoned the lady, said I'd made up my mind the part wasn't for me——"

"Damn you, Dex!" Eve's voice trembled as she swung toward Zach. Why wasn't he saying anything? Why wasn't he comforting her? "Zach, don't listen to him. None of that happened. He—he forced his way in here."

"And she says, 'Don't tell me that, Dex. Come on over and we'll talk about it.' She's been at me for weeks, holding out a contract I don't want with one hand and a bunch of promises with the other, if you know what I mean. So I came over, and she opened the door..." Dex flashed Zach a man-to-man smile. "Hey, man, I'm only human."

Zach's chest was constricted and his breathing was shallow. He'd been in fights before—hell, he'd fought his way through his teens and his first year in the Corps. He knew what it was like to feel adrenaline racing through his body.

But this was different. His muscles felt wound tight, like old-fashioned clock springs. He could hear the racing beat of his heart, feel the thud of his blood as it pounded through the veins in his temples. He needed to think, to sort out the facts from the fiction, but just now he was incapable of that and he knew it.

He was a man on the verge of explosion, and he relished it because that was all that might save his sanity.

He stepped toward Dex, a little smile angling across his mouth.

"You're wrong," he said, almost pleasantly. "You're not human. You're an insect." His arm shot back, flew forward, and his fist slammed into Dex's handsome, smiling face. "And I'm going to beat the crap out of you."

"Zach, no!" Sobbing, Eve threw herself at the two men. She pounded on Zach's shoulders, on his back, panting for him to stop.

Finally, when he knew the pain inside him would not go away, even if he mashed Dex to a pulp, Zach's hands fell to his sides.

Dex staggered back. There was blood on his face, on his shirt; he cringed as Zach stood over him, his hands on his hips, a look on his face that only a fool would have thought to defy.

Zach jerked his head toward the door.

"Get out," he said. "Get out of here, you scabby piece of maggot meat, and don't let me see your face ever again!"

Dex scrambled for the hall. Zach waited until he heard the front door slam shut, and then he turned to Eve.

His heart turned over. Lord, but she was beautiful. More beautiful than ever before, with her tearstained eyes and trembling lips.

More beautiful—and, perhaps, more treacherous.

"Zach," she whispered. Tears welled in her eyes and rolled down her cheeks. "Oh, Zach, it was so awful."

He could feel his muscles tense. He wanted to go to her, take her in his arms...

But he didn't move. "Tell me what happened here, Eve."

"I told you. Dex tried to—he tried to rape me."

"How did he get into the apartment?"

"He rang the bell. I thought it was you and——"

"How could you think it was me? I'd left. There was no reason to think I was coming back."

"Yes, but I thought—I thought..." Eve licked her lips. "I hoped you'd changed your mind," she whispered. "I was thinking how much I wanted you, how I wished I'd asked you to stay, and just at that moment, the bell rang."

"And you opened the door."

"Yes."

"Without looking? Without asking who it was?"

"Zach." She shook her head, trying to smile through her tears. "I know it was stupid. But I wanted it to be you so badly. I—I wanted—I wanted to tell you that I'm in love with you."

Her whispered words echoed in his head. She loved him. She loved him.

"Zach." Eve came toward him, still clutching the blanket to her. Her beautiful face was lifted, almost in supplication. "I know you have questions, but right now—right now, what I need is to have you take me in your arms and hold me. Just hold me, Zach, and tell me——"

"Tell me something first." Zach's voice was cold, almost without inflection. *Stop it,* an inner voice was saying, *stop it before it's too late....*

"Tell me he was lying. That you didn't invite him here."

He saw Eve's eyes widen. "But—but I *have* told you. I just described——"

"You told me what you want me to believe. What I want is the truth. Look me in the eye and say, 'Dex lied.'"

A cold hand seemed to wrap itself around Eve's heart.

"You don't believe me," she said softly.

"I didn't say that."

"Yes." Her breath caught. "Yes, you did. You want me to convince you that I'm innocent."

Zach's jaw tensed. "You have to admit, it doesn't look good. You, Dex, the clothing and the roses..."

"Zach. You can't believe——"

Zach spun away from her and slammed his hand against the wall. It was the hand he'd punched Dex with, the knuckles already bruised and hurting, but the ache, at least, cut through the nightmare of what was happening.

"I don't know what to believe," he roared. "Don't you see? I don't know what to believe!"

Silence filled the room. Eve stared at the man she had thought she loved, and then she took a deep breath.

"I told you once," she whispered, "I was never going to defend myself to you again."

"Eve, dammit——"

"Goodbye, Zach."

Darkness flashed in his eyes. "Eve..."

All her self-possession shattered in that instant. She flew toward him, still clinging to the blanket with one hand, and slammed her fist against his chest, over and over, until, at last, she fell back, sobbing.

"Get out of here. And don't ever come back!"

Zach looked at her. *God,* he thought, *dear God, what have I done?*

A terrible numbness swept over him.

He had done the right thing. The only thing.

He turned, made his way to the front door and walked out into the night.

It was amazing, how fast you could wrap things up if you really wanted to.

Zach phoned Ed Brubeck at home early Saturday morning, explained that he'd been called back to Boston on business.

"But my end of things is pretty much settled here," he said briskly, "and Eve's in charge of the creative stuff anyway, so if you'd just help me out, Ed, meet with her once a week or so to check out Triad's financial situation and then fax me the pertinent information..."

Brubeck said it would be no problem.

"It's just too bad you have to leave so suddenly," he said, and Zach hoped he sounded sincere when he said yes, yes, it certainly was.

He checked out of his hotel and stopped at the office on the way to the airport. He wrote Eve an impersonal memo, detailing some last-minute items he thought might need attention and informing her of the arrangement he'd made with Brubeck.

He reread it and frowned. There had to be more to say to a woman he'd been in love with...

Almost. Almost in love with.

He tossed aside his pencil, left the note on her desk, unsigned, and headed for the airport.

There were three planes heading east in the next hour. Unfortunately, none was destined for Boston. Two were headed for New York, one for Newark.

This was no time to be picky, Zach thought grimly, and bought a first-class ticket to Kennedy Airport, in New York.

"You'll have to hurry to make your flight, sir," the ticket agent told him.

Zach nodded, picked up his carryon bag and sprinted for the gate. Any time but this, he'd have figured on taking advantage of the New York touchdown to phone Grant in Manhattan, suggest they meet for a drink or dinner before he hopped a connecting flight to Logan, but the last thing he wanted right now was to sit down and pretend to be in a good mood.

How could he do that, after what had happened?

Zach handed his bag to the smiling flight attendant, put his portable computer on the empty seat beside him and stared blindly out the window.

To think that he, of all people, had been taken in by a woman like Eve.

It was infuriating.

But fury wasn't what he felt right now. What he felt was—was bruised. Hollow. He felt as if someone had reached inside him and torn out his heart.

Zach exhaled sharply. What he needed was to get back to the life he'd left behind him. A couple of crisp, New England autumn days and some time at his desk would blow the cobwebs out of his head, and then he'd be fine.

He'd be perfectly fine.

*   *   *

He jerked awake somewhere between Ohio and New York. The flight attendant was bending over him.

"Sorry to disturb you, Mr. Landon. But we're coming into some rough weather. The captain's asked all passengers to please put on their seat belts. Would you mind, sir?"

Zach shook his head, asked for a Bloody Mary and helped himself to a long look at the attendant's legs as she made her way up the cabin.

They were good legs. Great, actually. She had a nice bottom, too, and probably a face to go with the rest. He hadn't really noticed.

But what face would compare to Eve's? He never had decided what color her eyes really were, if they were the blue of sapphires or of the tropical sea. And her hair. That soft, silken, golden hair...

A scowl twisted across his face. He snatched up the newspaper lying beside him and buried his nose in it.

They landed in a driving rain, one that reminded him of the storm that had kept him and Eve trapped in that cabin in the mountains. Dammit, how long was this going to go on? he asked himself angrily as he headed for the Boston shuttle counter. There was no reason for *everything* to remind him of Eve, no reason to think of her at all.

The sooner he got home, the better.

But that, it seemed, would not be happening for a while. The rain was getting worse, and so were the winds accompanying it. The next shuttle for Boston had been canceled; passengers were asked to be patient and wait.

Be patient? Hell, that was the last thing he felt like being right now. And there was nothing worse than waiting around in an airport. He was hungry, too; an airline's idea of food and his had never been the same.

Zach looked at his watch. It was early evening. Grant was probably at home, having an early drink. How long would it take to get into the city? Thirty minutes, maybe? There wouldn't be much traffic, not on a rainy Sunday. He could pop by his brother's penthouse, have dinner with Grant and bring him up to date on Triad.

The business part of Triad, Zach thought with a little frown.

He started toward a bank of telephones, but all the booths were full. Well, he thought as he hurried toward the terminal exit, there was no reason to phone Grant. Neither he nor Grant nor Cade had ever been sticklers for formality.

Zach stepped outside, turned his collar up against the rain and signaled a waiting taxi. He got in, gave the driver Grant's Fifth Avenue address and settled back in his seat.

He probably wasn't fit company for anybody. His mood was lousy and his disposition rotten, but who better to let it out on than the brother who'd conned him into going out to California in the first place?

Besides, that was what family was for, Zach thought.

For the first time in hours, he smiled.

CHAPTER ELEVEN

IT HAD almost stopped raining by the time the cab dropped Zach off in front of Grant's apartment building. The air smelled clean and fresh.

Everything had improved, except for Zach's mood.

Damn, but he felt like such a fool. For a man to fall victim to the same kind of female barracuda not once but twice in his life was humiliating.

The lobby was empty. There'd always been a doorman on duty, but tonight the only sign of life was a half-empty coffee container and an open copy of the Sunday *Daily News*.

Not that it mattered. Months before, Grant had insisted on giving Zach a key to the private elevator that led to the penthouse.

The elevator doors sighed shut behind him and Zach leaned wearily against the wall as the car began to rise.

The shuttle flight being canceled hadn't been so bad. Truth was, he was looking forward to seeing Grant. They'd have a few drinks, talk about life in general and nothing in particular, maybe even have a few laughs—and laughs were certainly what he needed now.

Anything to keep him from thinking about Eve and how she'd suckered him in.

The elevator doors slid open on the penthouse foyer. Zach shook his head, smiling to himself as he always did at this first sight of his brother's home. It was big, and impressive, and almost painfully sterile.

Well, not as sterile as he'd remembered. There were bright flowers in the white vase that had once held an arrangement of something he'd always privately thought looked like a funeral offering. And there was a new painting on the wall, too, something so vivid it made his eyes water.

Zach put down his carryon. Man, it was certainly quiet.

"Grant?" He stepped farther into the apartment. "Mrs. Edison?"

A black shape came hurtling out of nowhere and threw itself at Zach's legs.

"Hey," he yelled.

He staggered back, regained his footing, stepped down on something soft and yielding and crashed to the floor. The thing he'd stepped on gave a bloodcurdling yowl, raced over his chest and disappeared into the living room.

Zach's heart was pounding. He sat up carefully and stared at the creature that had knocked him down. It was a dog, a mangy-looking mutt with funny ears, and it wasn't interested in ripping out his throat, it just wanted to lick the chin off his face.

He shoved the dog off him and got shakily to his feet. The thing he'd stepped on was glaring at him from the living room through yellow, feline eyes.

"Hell," Zach muttered.

It was quite a welcoming committee. A crazy dog and an insane cat.

A cat? A dog? Here, in a place where dust feared to settle?

Zach gave an unsteady laugh. Either he'd lost his mind or he was in the wrong apartment.

"What in hell's going on here?"

It wasn't the wrong place, Zach thought in amazement. There was Grant, coming down the stairs, wearing a scowl and a pair of blue pajama bottoms. And coming down the steps just behind him was a woman, her hand on his shoulder, wearing the pajama top.

A gorgeous woman.

"Zach?" A grin spread over Grant's face. "Zach," he repeated with delight, then turned to the woman. "Honey? Sweetheart, it's my brother."

Honey? Sweetheart?

Two Bloody Marys on the plane, Zach thought, that was all I had. Just two. Maybe three. Not enough to cause hallucinations.

Grant hurried toward him and clasped him by the shoulders.

"Hey, man, what a great surprise. How the heck are you?"

Zach looked down at himself. There was a tear in his Brooks Brothers jacket, a layer of cat fur on his chinos, and his chin felt as if it had been rubbed raw.

He laughed, something he'd never imagined doing again.

"I'm fine, considering that I've just been taken apart by a pair of bloodthirsty killers."

"Right." Grant laughed and turned to the woman, who was standing a few feet away, smiling hesitantly. "You hear that, darling? Annie and Sweetness just claimed their first victim."

The woman laughed. She had a sweet, musical voice. And she certainly was an eyeful, even in Grant's oversize pajama top. She had long black hair, violet eyes . . . She was lovely.

But not as lovely as Eve.

Zach cleared his throat. "Listen," he said, "I can see I've come at a bad time. So I'll collect my things and——"

Grant punched Zach lightly in the arm. "Stop being a fool," he said gruffly. "You're always welcome here. Anyway, I'm glad you guys have the chance to finally meet."

He smiled at the woman and held out his hand. She came toward him with an answering smile that made Zach's throat tighten.

"Zach," Grant said. He cleared his throat as the woman took his hand. "Zach, this is Crista Adams. She and I are going to be married."

A couple of hours later, after a terrific meal and some delightful conversation with the woman who was going to become his sister-in-law, Zach was standing on the terrace, a snifter of brandy in his hand.

It was chilly, but the view of Central Park lit up like a child's toy was spectacular.

The brothers were alone. Crista had excused herself and gone off upstairs, the dog at her heels and the cat in her arms.

"We have to be careful with the cat," Grant had said with a frown so serious Zach had almost cackled. "She's still not used to the terrace."

Now, Zach took another sip of brandy, looked at his brother and smiled.

"Well, you've certainly changed since the last time I saw you."

"Yeah, I guess I have. So have you, but not for the better."

Zach forced a smile to his lips. "I see you haven't changed entirely, pal. You're still about as subtle as a Sherman tank."

"I figure a man who's spent all this time on the Coast should have come back sporting a tan and a smile."

Zach shrugged his shoulders. "I've been too busy to work on a tan."

"Yeah, but a smile doesn't need any work at all."

Zach's eyebrows lifted. "Are you trying to make a point?"

"Only that you look terrible. And that I'd like to know the reason."

"Does there have to be a reason?" Zach said testily.

Grant shrugged. "For most people, yes." He took a swallow of his brandy. "Want to talk about it?"

Zach glared at him. "No," he said.

But he talked anyway. He said he'd gone out to California knowing what to expect. That he'd found just what he'd expected. That it hadn't kept him from making an absolute ass of himself anyway.

Grant kept nodding his head, saying, "Is that right?" and, "Uh-huh," and other brilliant things that meant nothing whenever Zach paused for breath. He didn't know what else to say. The problem was that for all his talking, his younger brother wasn't making a heck of a lot of sense.

He said a woman named Eve Palmer had wormed herself into a job she wasn't equipped for. Then he said she was the only person who could have done the job as well.

Bewildered, Grant tried to tell him that didn't make sense, but Zach was already off on another tangent, one that seemed to have no connection to the first, and this one turned out to be a shocker.

"My ex-wife was a bitch," he said bitterly. "Did you know that?"

"Well," Grant said, but Zach was already off and running.

He said his ex-wife had not just been coldhearted and conniving; he said she'd been unfaithful.

Grant was amazed, not by the antics of the former Mrs. Zachary Landon but by his brother's willingness to talk about them.

He and Cade had suspected what she was. But Zach had been married to her, and without proof, it had seemed wiser not to say anything.

Grant started to say as much, thought better of it and frowned when Zach switched back to talking about Eve Palmer.

"Man," he said, "I tell you, this broad's the worst piece of news you ever saw."

Grant stirred uneasily. Zach was looking at him. Was he supposed to make a comment?

"Ah, well," he said quickly, "no wonder Triad was in trouble."

Zach glared at him. "I just told you, she knows her stuff."

Grant nodded and cast a surreptitious glance into the living room. Where was Crista? She was a woman. Maybe she could figure out what in hell was going on here.

"She did give me a hard time, at first. Thought I was a bean counter."

Grant snorted. "You? A bean counter? I hope you set her straight."

"I did." Zach puffed out his breath. "What it comes to is, I made a mess of it."

The brothers' eyes met. Damn, Grant thought miserably, he's waiting for me to say something again....

"So," he said briskly, and got to his feet, "you made a mess out of telling this Palmer woman you weren't an accountant, and she became, ah, difficult to deal with?"

"Difficult to deal with might as well be her middle name," Zach grumbled.

Grant gave a deep sigh. "Listen, I'm trying to be helpful but I have to be honest, Zach, I can't be if you don't tell me what the hell was going on. I don't understand. Why was she such a bad piece of news? What was the problem? Why are you so upset?"

Zach looked at Grant. Half a dozen answers popped into his head.

Oh, hell, he thought. He swallowed the last of his brandy, put the glass down and told the truth.

"Because I fell in love with her," he said.

The words hung between the men, as sharp as the autumn air. Grant reached out and squeezed his brother's shoulder.

"Okay," he said. "That says it all."

"No!" Zach slammed his fist against the railing. "Dammit, you don't understand! I loved her, but she didn't love me."

Grant sighed. "She broke things off when you told her you loved her?"

"No." Zach's mouth turned down. "I never told her."

"You never——"

"No, and it's a damned good thing I didn't." His jaw knotted. "I——I found her with another man."

"Hell." Grant's heart went out to his brother. It wasn't fair, he thought. He and Cade had both found happiness. Why shouldn't Zach? "Listen, if that's the kind of bitch she is——"

In an instant, Grant found himself standing on his toes, nose to nose with Zach, who was holding him by the front of his shirt and glaring at him as if he wanted to kill him.

"Don't call her that," Zach said through his teeth.

The brothers stared at each other, and then Grant began to laugh. After a couple of seconds, Zach laughed, too. He let go of Grant's shirt, smoothed the wrinkles and grinned.

"Sorry."

"Think nothing of it, pal." Grant punched him lightly in the arm. "It just proves that some things never change. You've still got the disposition of a bad-tempered rhino."

"Yeah." Zach's smile faded. "Man, oh, man," he muttered, "I am a mess, aren't I?"

"You're in love, you jerk."

"No." Zach shook his head. "Not anymore."

"Trust me," Grant said dryly. "You've got all the symptoms." He cleared his throat. "Listen, are you sure you, ah, you found her with some guy? I mean, some-times what looks like one thing really is another.''

''Yeah. That's pretty much what she said.''

''What do you mean?''

Zach sighed. ''She claimed the guy was forcing himself on her, but——''

''But?''

''But, I'd seen her give this guy the come-on before. Look, it's a long story but the bottom line is that she's one of those dames who trades. You know, this for that.''

''Like your ex.''

''Yes. No. Eve is—oh, hell, she's nothing like my ex. Eve is gentle and sweet. But tough. I mean, she's a strong woman, inside, where it counts. And she's so beautiful...'' Zach groaned and ran his hands through his hair. ''I think I've gone nuts.''

''Let me get this straight,'' Grant said slowly. ''She's gentle. Sweet. Strong inside. Am I right so far?''

''What's your point?''

''Stay with me, Okay? She's all these things, plus beautiful. And you fell in love with her. You're still in love with her—and yet you didn't believe her when she said she wasn't screwing around with some other guy?''

''Grant, you're making it sound so simple but I tell you, I saw her!''

''Did you?'' Grant's eyes met Zach's. ''Or did you see only what you expected to see?''

Zach's brows drew together. ''And what, exactly, is that supposed to mean?''

''It means,'' Grant said gruffly, ''that you're as big a fool as Cade and me. It means not a one of us had the brains to figure out that the real Landon legacy wasn't Landon Enterprises at all."

"Listen, man, I don't know what you're talking about."

Grant sighed. "Sure you do. You just haven't faced it yet."

"Look, thanks for trying to help me, but——"

"Some fathers teach their sons to play ball or to fish, but the lesson we got from ours cut a lot deeper." Grant's mouth thinned. "The old man taught us never to believe in anybody or anything—especially love."

"Come on, Grant. Maybe that goes for you and Cade, but not me. I was the only one of us who got married, remember?"

Grant folded his arms over his chest. "And look at the woman you chose," he said grimly. "A wonderful example of femininity, if ever there was one."

"So I made a mistake. But I corrected it."

"You damned fool," Grant snapped, "Cade and I suspected it the first time we met her. She was all wrong for you. There was never a chance in a billion your marriage could have worked."

Zach's face whitened with anger. "Why didn't you say something?"

"Because suspicion is not proof," Grant said calmly, "because we loved you too much to hurt you, and because we hoped to hell we were wrong, that's why." His eyes narrowed. "And because you wouldn't have listened. You've always been the most hot-tempered, pigheaded idiot imaginable."

The brothers glowered at each other for a moment, and then Zach gave a choked laugh.

"You sound like her," he said.

"Eve?"

"Yes. She called me pigheaded, too."

Grant smiled. "I like the lady already."

"Yes. You would like her. Would have, I mean. I mean, you'd have been fooled, same as me. You'd have thought she was everything wonderful, everything a man could want..."

There was a long, terrible silence, and then Zach groaned and sank down into a wicker chair.

"I failed her," he said brokenly. "She loved me, she needed me, and I failed her."

Grant looked at his brother's stricken face. "Then go to her," he said softly.

"I can't. She won't want to see me. She told me never to come back."

Grant's hand tightened on Zach's shoulder. "Go to her," he said. "Tell her you love her. Put your heart on the line." He smiled. "Isn't it worth the risk?"

Zach looked up. "It'll be the worst risk I've ever taken," he said softly. "If I lose her..."

Grant put out his right hand, palm up. "Deadeye Defenders never lose," he said.

A slow smile eased across Zach's lips. He rose, clasped Grant's hand. The brothers looked at each other and then they embraced.

"Good luck," Grant called, as Zach hurried from the terrace.

Eve sat in her kitchen, drinking the worst coffee anyone had ever made, but she couldn't complain since she had made it.

She sighed. Apparently she'd lost count of how many measures of coffee she'd put into the pot. Not that it mattered. The stuff was hot and maybe the caffeine would jolt her into some kind of functional behavior.

Not that she had any reason to be functional. Today was Sunday. The fact that she'd paced the floor most of the night, that she hadn't slept in hours, wouldn't matter. She could just sit here and pretend to read the newspapers all day, and nobody would know the difference.

Except she didn't really want to read. Or drink this coffee. Or do much of anything.

With a sigh, she put down her cup, let the paper fall to the floor and got to her feet.

No matter how she tried, she kept thinking about what had happened Friday night. For all she knew, she would never stop thinking about it.

Not about Dex. He was exactly what Zach had called him, a piece of maggot meat, and she was only sorry she hadn't gotten the chance to clobber him with a shoe, but he wasn't worth thinking about any more.

It was Zach who haunted her thoughts, Zach and what a fool she'd made of herself over him.

She had loved him. Loved him desperately, even let herself begin to think—to hope—that he loved her, too.

Her throat constricted. Oh, yes. Yes, Zach had really loved her, so much that when she'd needed him most, he'd abandoned her.

She'd been fine, right after it had happened, so enraged and filled with righteous indignation that she'd let it out everywhere, even on Mrs. Harmon.

Remembering, she had to smile at how she'd banged on the old woman's door.

"Where were you when I needed you?" she'd demanded.

She'd let the anger out in more useful ways, too, first cleaning all traces of Dex from the apartment, then scrubbing herself—again—until her skin felt raw, finally collapsing onto the sofa and tumbling into exhausted sleep.

And that was when the worst ache of her life had replaced the anger. She'd dreamed, dreamed of Zach, and wasn't that pathetic? Dreamed that he'd come back, that he'd pleaded for her to love him, that he'd begged her to understand that he'd been wrong and she'd gone into his arms...

The doorbell rang. Eve didn't bother moving. Whoever it was would go away. The bell rang again.

"There's nobody home," she called.

Silence. After a moment, she sighed, sat down at the table and put her head in her arms.

It was ridiculous to sit here and feel sorry for herself. Zach wasn't worth it. She knew that now. She'd known it all the time.

The phone rang. She ignored it. The answering machine would take the call. She heard the ringing stop, heard the distant sound of her own recorded message.

"Eve? Eve, it's Zach. Please, please, pick up the phone."

Eve shot to her feet and raced to the machine.

"Eve, please. Talk to me."

"No," she whispered. But Zach couldn't hear her; only the machine was listening. "No," she repeated, and stabbed out her hand to silence his voice.

"Darling Eve, I love you."

A sob rose in her throat. There they were, the words she'd longed to hear. But they'd come too late.

"There's so much I should have told you, Eve."

What could he possibly tell her that would take away the pain?

"Sweetheart, I never knew what love meant, until you came into my life."

"It's too late," she whispered to the machine.

"You came into my life, darling, and I—I was terrified." Zach's laughter was harsh and bitter. "Me, the guy who'd spent his life looking for risks... I took one look at you and I was afraid, because—because I knew, in my heart, that to admit the truth, that I'd fallen in love with you, that I needed you, would strip my soul bare."

Tears spilled down Eve's cheeks, but she didn't move. If only it had been true. Oh, if only...

"Darling." She heard the sharp intake of his breath. "I'm at the corner, at that funny little place where we had that awful breakfast, remember? Meet me there. Let me take you in my arms and tell you how much I adore you."

Eve turned away, her hands at her lips. *Zach,* she thought, *Zach, how can I believe you?*

"Let me take you in my arms and ask you to be my wife, Eve. Do you hear me? Eve, please! Tell me you'll marry me, tell me you love me..."

Laughter and sobs broke from Eve's lips. She grabbed the phone and put it to her ear.

"Of course, I love you," she said in a choked voice. "I've loved you since you tried to kill Horace the Wonder Horse!"

In a phone booth down the street, Zach closed his eyes, breathed a prayer of thanks to whatever gods might be listening, and smiled.

"Who'd ever have believed I'd have a lucky talisman named Horace the Wonder Horse?" he said, leaning back against the wall of the booth.

"Zach?" Eve took a deep breath. "There are things I should have told you, too. About—about my foster father, and how he tried—how he tried to molest me." She had not said the words aloud in so many years. Oh, what a relief it was to say them now. "But no one believed me," she said shakily. "He called me a—a whore, and I swore I'd never trust anyone again."

Zach cursed himself for a fool and made a silent vow he would spend the rest of his life making up for Eve's pain.

"Trust me, my love," he said. "Give me your heart, and I swear I'll cherish it. Eve—will you marry me?"

"Yes. Oh, yes. I love you, Zach. Only you. You were the first, the only one..."

The phone dropped from Eve's hand. She ran to the door, flung it open and flew down the steps to the street. She saw Zach, already racing toward her. His arms opened wide when he saw her, and she flung herself into them.

"Eve," he said, "Eve..."

He whirled her around and around while he kissed her, tasting the sweetness of her mouth and the salt of her tears, knowing that some of those tears were surely his.

"Marry me," he whispered, and she laughed and put her hands on either side of his face and brought his mouth, his dear, sweet mouth, down to hers again.

"Yes," she said, "yes, oh, yes..."

Behind them, a window opened. An old lady looked out. She watched as the lovers embraced, and she began to smile.

* * * * *

Now you've enjoyed Zach's and Eve's romance, please look out for Kyra's and Antonio's story, coming next month in SPRING BRIDE by the same author.

Coming Next Month

HARLEQUIN PRESENTS®

#1821 UNWANTED WEDDING Penny Jordan
(Top Author)
Rosy had to be married within three months. Guard Jamieson was successful, sexy—and single. With no other candidate available to walk her down the aisle, it looked as if Rosy would have to accept Guard's offer to help her out.

#1822 DEADLY RIVALS Charlotte Lamb
(Book Two: SINS)
When Olivia first met Max she was utterly captivated. But Max was her father's business enemy and she was forbidden to see him again. Four years later she agreed to marry Christos, Max's nephew. Then Max returned to claim her....

#1823 TWO'S COMPANY Carole Mortimer
(9 TO 5)
Juliet's boss has left her half his company but she has to share it with Liam, his son, who is sure that she seduced his father. Nor does she want him to know that she was engaged to his despised younger brother. Will he find out her dark secret?

#1824 A SAVAGE BETRAYAL Lynne Graham
(This Time, Forever)
Mina and Cesare had met again, four years after he rejected her as a gold-digging tramp! Now he was determined to marry her, but only to pursue his revenge on Mina.

#1825 SPRING BRIDE Sandra Marton
(Landon's Legacy: Book 4)
Kyra's father's legacy would allow her to assert her independence. Antonio would help her—but at a price! He wanted to own her completely—and if she succumbed Kyra knew she would never be free again.

#1826 PERFECT CHANCE Amanda Carpenter
(Independence Day)
Mary's life was reasonably happy—until the day Chance Armstrong walked into it! He was offering her the perfect chance for a lot of excitement and the most exciting challenge of all.... He asked Mary to marry him!

Take 4 bestselling love stories FREE

Plus get a FREE surprise gift!

Special Limited-time Offer

Mail to Harlequin Reader Service®

3010 Walden Avenue
P.O. Box 1867
Buffalo, N.Y. 14240-1867

YES! Please send me 4 free Harlequin Presents® novels and my free surprise gift. Then send me 6 brand-new novels every month, which I will receive months before they appear in bookstores. Bill me at the low price of $2.90 each plus 25¢ delivery and applicable sales tax, if any*. That's the complete price and a savings of over 10% off the cover prices—quite a bargain! I understand that accepting the books and gift places me under no obligation ever to buy any books. I can always return a shipment and cancel at any time. Even if I never buy another book from Harlequin, the 4 free books and the surprise gift are mine to keep forever.

106 BPA A3UL

Name	(PLEASE PRINT)	
Address	Apt. No.	
City	State	Zip

This offer is limited to one order per household and not valid to present Harlequin Presents® subscribers. *Terms and prices are subject to change without notice. Sales tax applicable in N.Y.

UPRES-696

BRIDE'S BAY RESORT

UNLOCK THE DOOR TO GREAT ROMANCE AT BRIDE'S BAY RESORT

Join Harlequin's new across-the-lines series, set in an exclusive hotel on an island off the coast of South Carolina.

Seven of your favorite authors will bring you exciting stories about fascinating heroes and heroines discovering love at Bride's Bay Resort.

Look for these fabulous stories coming to a store near you beginning in January 1996.

Harlequin American Romance #613 in January
Matchmaking Baby by Cathy Gillen Thacker

Harlequin Presents #1794 in February
Indiscretions by Robyn Donald

Harlequin Intrigue #362 in March
Love and Lies by Dawn Stewardson

Harlequin Romance #3404 in April
Make Believe Engagement by Day Leclaire

Harlequin Temptation #588 in May
Stranger in the Night by Roseanne Williams

Harlequin Superromance #695 in June
Married to a Stranger by Connie Bennett

Harlequin Historicals #324 in July
Dulcie's Gift by Ruth Langan

Visit Bride's Bay Resort each month wherever
Harlequin books are sold.

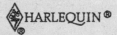

HARLEQUIN®

BBAYG

Where there's a will there's a way...
for four charismatic characters to find love

LANDON'S LEGACY

by Sandra Marton
Book 4: #1825 SPRING BRIDE

When Charles Landon dies, he leaves behind a
different legacy for each of his children: for vulnerable
Kyra Landon this means a passionate encounter with
Antonio Rodrigo Cordoba del Rey—a man way
out of her league?

For Cade, Grant, Zach and Kyra, Landon's Legacy
is the key to their happiness—and very special love
matches that will last a lifetime!

Harlequin Presents: you'll want to know
what happens next!

Available in July wherever Harlequin books are sold.

HARLEQUIN ◆ PRESENTS®

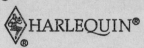